The
Last Peacock

The
Last Peacock

ALLAN MASSIE

THE BODLEY HEAD

LONDON   SYDNEY

TORONTO

FOR ALISON AGAIN

The author thanks the Scottish Arts Council
for a bursary which helped him to write this book.

British Library Cataloguing
in Publication Data
Massie, Allan
The last peacock.
823'.9'1F   PR6063.A79L/
ISBN 0-370-30261-3

© Allan Massie 1980
Printed in Great Britain for
The Bodley Head Ltd
9 Bow Street, London WC2E 7AL
by Redwood Burn Ltd, Trowbridge and Esher
Set in Monotype Imprint
by Gloucester Typesetting Co Ltd
First published 1980

The
Last Peacock

I

'Belinda,' comes the old woman's voice from the high bed, 'where is the girl?'

The voice has lost definition, can no longer punctuate, and Belinda, standing by the window, is uncertain for a moment whether she is the girl referred to or whether perhaps her name is in the vocative, the girl being other.

She runs her hands over her buttocks, fingers free on the green velvet of her trousers, and looks out still from the long curtain-fringed window. Dark-leaved rhododendrons gloom in the afternoon and their mauve-pink flowers run wetly. A peacock picks its way between the croquet hoops and pegs which are forlorn, at all angles, the bird's blue-sheened neck moving up and down. Belinda pushes back the blonde straggle of hair but does not turn towards the bed nor answer her grandmother. She extends the forefinger of her left hand to the window, tracing the raindrops coursing down outside.

'Erred and strayed from Thy ways . . . I should like a cup of tea.'

She won't drink it, thinks Belinda, in a moment she will forget that she asked for it.

She lights, even in the sickroom, a cigarette. There is a smell of tobacco smoke throughout the house, blending with potpourri, roses and old age. Old age of dog and cat as well as woman.

Belinda looks beyond the trees which fringe the lawn to another country where the sea is deep blue, rocks black and the azaleas in bloom.

Grace in the high bed is smaller than before, her face tobacco-wrinkled, wisps of grey hair, her night-gown yellowing. A ruby still gleams on her finger. Cushions prop her up.

On the table to the left of the bed (the one which is not used for medicine-bottles, glasses and rose-patterned tea-cups) photographs stand in array, measuring out the stages of a life. Grace at fifteen in a tea-gown, curls escaping from a bonnet to dance on her cheek. Grace in a bathing suit, Juan-les-Pins 1923, chase me into the sea, roll me on the sand, yes, ducky, I will have a gasper, that was luvly, but . . . off, off, off . . . to tea for two, by the light most any night . . . Grace in her wedding-dress. The parish church, soldiers of the kilted regiment holding swords over Grace, who wilts enticingly on the arm of their major, whose brushed-up moustache already indicates his astonishing capacity for getting things wrong. That, and the boiled eye, which speaks of limited vocabulary. Grace Madonna and child . . . Uncle Alastair, well Uncle Alastair, Belinda sighs even now for Uncle Alastair; what are the tangled threads of consanguinity that can . . . It is better not to think of Uncle Alastair who has been dead since Normandy, whom she never met, whose photographs from the age of twelve, story intimated over the years, seem to have fore-ordained, fixed in a rhythm insistent as the bolero, so many errors. If, Belinda sighs to the peacock, they are indeed errors.

Alastair at sixteen perhaps, in cricket flannels, throat exposed by open-necked shirt. Belinda can smell the sweat across the decades, the insidious call of athleticism hand in hand with softness. Because it is not really Alastair, whom she never met but who set the pattern.

'China tea with lemon. I always drink China tea with lemon.'

There are moments when Grace becomes Belinda; for Belinda.

'Would you really like some tea? I'll make a pot.'

'Ring for it, dear, the bell-pull's by the bedhead. My back, I can't reach it, oh my back.'

Belinda hesitates. There is no one to answer the bell, and anyway, she has never in the twenty years she has known the house heard it ring. As her brother Andrew said, 'You could write a paper, darling, if you were a beastly little student, on how we experienced the simultaneous extinction of servants and functioning bells to summon them. All over the country you can find boxes of kitchen bells and none of them work.

6

Rum. It's an interesting question though it would, darling, be, of course, no denying it, a bloody boring paper. That's sociology for you.'

So Belinda hesitates. Then she pulls the bell-rope—the silken threads are separating, a gold thread and a purple one cling to her hand. Grace sinks back, or seems to, though in fact all that happens is that her moment of radiated satisfaction makes her seem to sink.

The twilight deepens. Belinda plugs in an electric kettle, kneeling beside it, flowered shirt riding up to reveal flesh, beach-coloured in the dullness. She carefully checks that there is enough water in the kettle and is back on her feet, rising like a fountain in a Roman garden.

There is a silence in the room until the kettle approaching the boil begins its roar. Belinda, by the window again, ignores it until clouds of steam and a rattling lid attract reluctant attention. She kneels, heats the teapot, empties it in the wash-basin, puts in black, long-leaved tea and pours the water. All this without awareness; a thing that does itself. After a few minutes, she pours two cups, one only half-full because the tremor of Grace's hand is such that she can only manage it this way. She carries it over to the bed. Grace is asleep.

Belinda had arrived the week before last; in evening sunshine. Foxgloves outside the window showed her carriage had overrun the platform. An old habit of the train, somehow forgotten. She stood, Londony-forlorn in elegance, high-heeled on the high step, dismayed by the drop. Just about to throw her case down and jump, noticed the station-master, everything country station-master should be, always in her experience had been, though doubtless a different man yet not to be distinguished from his predecessor, waving with authority. The engine was to reverse, let her descend, to a scented platform.

Since Perth, a station diminished yet still a gateway, her pulse had beaten faster. She had felt a little sick and hollow. Skirt too well-cut, hair too shining even after a day in the train. Homecoming a time for a mask. And when she had entered the restaurant car to find it not at all a restaurant car but a place where muffins were unthinkable and only plastic-cased sandwiches available, childhood died again.

She could hear birds she couldn't identify as the train began to back, doubtless reluctant . . . One hand steadied her case, the other lightly touched her lips. Ponies in a field on one side of the track cantered to a river she couldn't see.

Except for the station-master there was only one figure on the platform who, turning as if from contemplation of the station yard deserted but for an olive Range Rover, revealed himself as her cousin, Martin.

They didn't know how to greet each other, or rather she didn't and Martin said nothing. Words made perhaps super-fluous by his checked tweed jacket, checked tweed cap and cavalry twill trousers, all cutting off communication, for how —Belinda didn't work this out or rather it never struck her till much later—could words fly backwards? She gave him her case. Such a figure, such a platform, existed to be given cases. But she held on to the bag that contained her clart.

She thanked the station-master who affected to know her, perhaps did, but said something instead to Martin about agricultural matters. Not apparently worth acknowledgement beyond a nod. May have been a grunt. Belinda couldn't be sure.

Intolerable silence of broken years in the Range Rover, made worse by the snuffling of the labrador.

At last,

'I expected Colin,' she said.

'Oh, yes?'

'But it's good of you to have come.'

'Now is the time for all good men . . . a bloody awful party though, if you don't mind my saying so.'

'Mind, why should I?'

'Never minded anything, did you?'

'Not even . . .' What's what, she'd been going to say, but it wasn't somehow possible to revive old jokes, which had never been without their taste of vinegar.

8

'How are Jill and the children?'—unable to remember names.

'Good of you to ask,' he said with a lightness that was new.

'They must be getting on. It's terrible, I'm so lost.'

'They don't grow younger. Colin's in the pub. We're stopping for him.'

'Christ, what a bugger he is.'

'Oh aye, that's Colin.'

She began, one part of her, to relax, while simultaneously she felt emptier at thought of Colin. But she could take in the soft-mannered . countryside, pheasants in the evening parkland, beeches, chestnuts, elms and oaks, glimpses of the river, and, through a gap in the trees, the blue hills only five or six miles away.

'Not his fault really, lost his licence you know. Part of country life now, Bel.'

'What about as a passenger?'

And they both laughed.

'Only so far as a passenger,' said Martin.

'So far being the Graham Arms?'

'In one . . . give the lady the coconut,'—which wasn't Martin, but Colin.

She could see him though the open door of the public bar. Grey in his hair, only in streaks but grey. Sitting cross-legged on the bar stool, tweed suit (Lovat of course) ever so well cut but a touch shabby. Paid for, Colin? Undoubtedly. By Colin? Undoubtedly not. Some time ago anyway. Spurt of what she could accept as love.

'Lazy sodding swine, not to come to the station. Typical, to leave it to Martin.'

'Got you a drink, sis.' Colin, to prove it, handed a gin-and-tonic. 'Division of labour, secret of Henry Ford's success in life.'

'Doesn't work for everyone, does it, ducky?'

. . . Colin is so Colin there is nothing Belinda can say which would say what she feels. She is given to self-analysis none of which is ever on view and so she is aware of this, and to feel what you say is not the same as to say what you feel.

9

So Belinda is also aware of herself as an image projected, oh very decoratively, on others, for their consumption; what is not projected is only in part even more Belinda. She is undoubtedly her image and she cannot imagine herself ugly; even though she often says, 'Christ, what a hag I look . . .'

Colin, himself also drinking gin-and-tonic, gave Belinda the smile of a child conspirator.

'Well,' he said, 'the North is pretty northern, the old girl's dying and it's family reunion time, jolly family reunion. How do you think she looks, Martin?'

'Great.'

'Strong, silent. It's true, ducky, she's really dying this time, not before you might say, and, tell you a secret, it's not even certain it's going to be a great fifth act. No fifth acts in Scottish life, no third ones either I sometimes say.'

But though Colin said northern, the hotel bar in the early summer evening sunshine, with the labrador panting saliva, wasn't the grim North of imagination. Something suspended, time held still, like the particles of dust lit up by the sinking sun. Along the bar two farm labourers, one with the bottoms of his trousers tied with string, did not look at Belinda, Colin, Martin, though they had recognized her on entry. It was politeness. In response, Colin's death-talk shivered the conventions.

'I had a letter from Julie,' Colin said, surprising her; it wasn't his way ever to vouchsafe information at all affecting him, blood more easily to be drawn from stones. Her first thought was that he must be concealing something else. This news was bait for distraction.

'How is the slut?'

'She thinks I should pay her two thousand a year.'

Dead-pan.

'Good joke, eh?'

'Hilarious.'

Martin, restless, chunked coins, attracting Colin's attention to the absolute imperative of re-charging glasses. Did the barman—not a native (new proprietor?)—look doubtful?

'Mr Smith, you haven't met my sister. I'm sorry. This is

my glamorous sister, not the successful one. Mr Smith's knowledge of our family ramifications could be the talk of the County. If he cared. But sometimes,' he leant over confidingly, 'sometimes, ducky, I think it exceeds his interest. And he keeps it all to himself . . . On the slate, is that all right?'

'No, no,' said Belinda, 'I'll pay . . . let me . . . why not?'

'Why not indeed?'

The envelope Mr Smith, one of those nondescript types who find themselves running Scottish country pubs, their only qualification (in itself possibly a desirable one in the circumstances) being a bleak moroseness consonant with the decor and ambience, had produced seemed well covered with figures. Ought she to offer to settle up? Till his cheque came in? Probably not. Perhaps the mention of Julie's demands was intended to impress Mr Smith; it seemed unlikely he was impressible.

Martin had refused a drink. It had taken a moment for Belinda to realize this.

'You want us to get a move on?'

'Martin is a man of affairs.'

She had never understood why Martin tolerated Colin. Couldn't surely be cousinship, propinquity and habit overcoming innate antipathy. Could it be perhaps that he still, even now, responded to a certain style, to Colin's debonair assumption of a superiority that didn't have to be earned; and that this superiority was somehow maintained in the face of experience that made nonsense of it? Did Martin's inner voice, if Martin had an audible inner voice, say to him: Colin's failure mocks your success—your decent success? Martin might say, and did say, often enough, 'What a shit your brother is', but there was always a thin note of envy in his voice. And nights when Martin shut himself up, if they still happened, and drank a bottle of brandy, always suggested to her a thwarted anarchism. Did he see in Colin the courage that chose its own route to hell?

Nevertheless Martin got them out of the pub, which Belinda was happy to leave, and there was no suggestion from Colin that Martin should go home and they could take a taxi. It might be there was nowadays no taxi to take.

'I won't come in,' he said, 'it's too late. I'll come over tomorrow.'

'Yes, Martin is a man of affairs,' Colin repeated.

'How are you really?'

'So-so. Have you seen our mother?'

'Last week. I told you on the telephone.'

'Don't think so.'

'She won't come up, not yet.'

'Bloody soon it'll be over.'

'She has important meetings.'

It was lovely in the evening air. Simple as that. Lovely. They stood in the porch of the house which had once been a manse and was large, rambling, two-staircased, a house for children's hide-and-seek, and Belinda breathed in real air.

'How good,' she said. 'What have you been doing?'

'This and that.'

'Frowsting and slumming, I expect. Bet you haven't been doing anything.'

'I keep myself occupied. The daily grind, common task.'

'I see, unremitting toil.'

'That sort of thing.'

The line of talk, light though it was, was enough to make him pick up her suitcase and carry it upstairs to her room.

'See you downstairs. I got some wine. Have you eaten?'

'No,' she said.

'Nothing but filth on the train. See you in the kitchen then.'

The bedroom is all shadows and for a moment she doesn't switch on a light but goes to the window and stands there. There is a touch of mist in the sky now, a sound of water and bird-song. The sharp cackle of pheasant and, as if in response, from the beech trees where the garden ends and the ground drops to the river, the scream of a peacock; ridiculous fancy. A peacock in a manse garden. The peacock is the emptiest of birds, all show, always thought so. In the shadows—and the bedroom is darkened by heavy brown velvet curtains, never wholly withdrawn—mahogany furniture is islanded. A ewer and basin stand still on the marble washstand. Belinda switches on the light to look again at the engraving above it, where shepherdesses in Arcady converse with goat-footed herds; intimations of sexuality tremble between them that will never be translated into action. Yet the action is already there. Belinda plays with a cord from her collar, unaware of doing so. In the background a ruined temple may be obligatory—no such scene should be without one. The grass the shepherdesses recline on is close cropped; vegetation threatens to destroy the temple. A little further off a lone Corinthian column supports a boy who himself wears a garland of what look like acanthus leaves.

Belinda washes, that is she dabs a cold cloth on her face and then applies cream.

The kitchen gloomed, stone-flagged, vaulted, big-tabled, cavernous. The tables had an elemental quality. They were solid and rough-hewn country tables with no hint of varnish. The room looked out on a mean yard with a pile of wood that had not been disturbed in a long time; open-doored cellars were built into the hill-side; half-feral cats lurked at the entrances.

Colin busied himself opening a bottle of wine. No need of a corkscrew for this quality. He poured himself a glass, red and sharp. He put a pork pie on a plate and ran some water over lettuce leaves.

Laurels shaded the side window; rhododendrons beyond and then gorse.

It was going to rain; clouds gathered as the summer disintegrated.

Colin, preparations complete, sat and waited. A clock ticked. A tabby cat purred. The first drops of rain streaked the window.

'There's not much to eat,' he said to his sister entering.

'Doesn't matter. I brought some coffee from Whittard's.'

'Just as well. Highland village prices here, for ersatz.'

Silence hung between them, watchful. Belinda and Colin, Colin and Belinda, the pall of inertia, both sitting now, thinking, turning over conversations, while she stroked the cat just behind its right ear, then round and under, along the line of its purring jawbone; while he nursed the wine he hadn't touched since she came into the room just as he poured himself a second tumbler.

They could talk of other members of the family. Thoughts could then remain where they were, locked up.

He said, 'See quite a bit of Martin, time to time.'

'He seems all right.'

'Well, nothing ever is all right for Martin. Ought to know that. Never has been. Secret of his success.'

'No, but he seems himself. Is he, would you say, a success? In what sense?'

'Just being Martin not enough for success? Perhaps not. He's become a political force, Martin.'

'Martin, how?'

'That you know is one of the surest signs of middle age, when you find your contemporaries becoming politicians.'

'But Martin's not a politician—he's a farmer, nothing but a . . .'

'Chairman of the local branch of the NFU of course but it's not that, Chairman of the local Unionists, or Conservatives as they seem to call themselves now. Rum to change when their raison d'être seems to be to preserve the Union.'

'Good heavens!'

'You truly didn't know? Thing is, you see, the local SNP, probably you wouldn't have heard in Fulham, but thing is, really frightful chaps. Natch class solidarity obliges even soi-disant noblesse to . . . very boring but has its amusing side . . . and so our mother won't come up?'

'Not just yet,' she says.

'As far as I'm concerned . . .' but instead of saying what as far as he is concerned Colin drinks some wine and lights a cigarette.

'Jill,' he says, 'wasn't at all pleased to hear you were coming. She still expects you one day to ride into the sunset with Martin.'

Belinda doesn't appear to hear this. She looks blankly into the twilight, lips parted and fingers running on her thigh.

14

Colin thinks, The difference between lips parted and mouth open, and why don't they say the same thing and is it objective or subjective?

'Mind you,' he said, 'she looks more like a *Gruppenunterführer* than ever. This really is appalling muck, this wine.'

'Why drink it then?'

'One must drink something and till things look up ...'

'Will things look up?'

'They always have ...'

Belinda begins to make some coffee. She is not exactly wondering why she has come, because she knows the answer to that one and there was nothing else to do, though that of course has never stopped Colin or herself from doing just that, but she would like to scream. It is terrible to be standing in a twilight cavern and wanting to scream.

Colin doesn't say, You see, *sorella mia*, we are two of a kind. I fill you with horror because you see in my indifference your own being. Of course we can always laugh, twin-soul of mine, but that is all we can do. No I forgot; we can also sneer. And beneath our languid accidie what lurks? Fear of the gnawing worm.

But he doesn't say any of this and yet the words thud in his mind. They thud with a recurrence and a resonance and he can never be sure he hasn't said them though he knows his lips are still. Is there meaning yet conveyed?

Belinda says, 'There are spiders' webs ... does no one clean now?'

'Oh, webs. Jessie's not one for webs.'

'She still comes?'

'Oh yes, don't know what we would do without Jessie, lazy incompetent slut but invaluable treasure.'

And he sips more wine. It is in protest, which he recognizes as also recognition, that Belinda goes to a cupboard, emerges with a long-stemmed feather duster and attacks the cobwebs. Such cleaning is easy.

Martin has not gone home, which is something he does these days as late as late as he can find an excuse for the delays; and for a farmer excuses are not hard to find. However he has supplemented them by his recent engagement in active politics and tonight he is not driving his Land-Rover up the hill track to walk among his Blackface sheep, or strolling with a stick in the haughs by the river among the soft-breathing, warm-flanked Charolais, but attending an Extraordinary General Meeting of the local Conservative Association. They are to debate and, it is thought, pass a motion of no confidence in their Member of Parliament.

This is itself extraordinary but there are fears that he will not be able to retain the seat against a rising Nationalist challenge.

The Member of Parliament is not expected to attend the debate. It is believed that his supporters have persuaded him that he stands a better chance in his absence. There is perhaps a certain illogicality here for if he survives the night, will he be expected to absent himself during the election campaign also? There are those who think this might be a good idea, but they are not generally numbered among his supporters.

The Member of Parliament thinks himself a wit but is only a wag. He wears a kilt which his buttocks cannot support. He has been photographed with his feet in a mustard bath.

All these things are held against him.

On the other hand he is a scourge of Socialism. He deplores public waste and says aloud what many of his constituents think, that unemployment is idleness and trade unionists traitors.

It will be a close run thing and Martin, who is respected, may turn the balance.

He has a whisky with the local vet. The vet says, 'The bloody man makes us look fools . . .'

'Fools to elect him.'

'That's what I mean, he can blether to his heart's content, and I don't mind admitting he comes out with things I'm very glad to hear said in public, but . . .'

'He's a wee spouter . . .'

Martin buys another round . . . six double whiskies mean

16

little to him, his Charolais fetch such prices these days . . . the vet may be glad he is not paying for this one, since others have joined them seeing Martin is on the bell. Now in these circumstances the Member of Parliament would go on standing his hand but Martin will not put his in his pocket again till he's been bought drinks by everyone. Since that would come to more whisky than he will drink tonight, this is the last round he will buy.

'All art,' says Colin, still in the kitchen drinking bad wine, 'all art,' he says with the decorum of his tweed suit, 'is disposable rubbish. That is the sick thought of a sick mind, but yet I speak it. Maybe it didn't used to be, historically indeed it evidently wasn't, but now it is. Conditioned for example by destructive painting how can we view Titian as Ruskin saw him? I can't remember, which is immaterial, whether Ruskin admired him. That is immaterial too. It doesn't change the meaning of what I say.'

Maybe Belinda, sitting on the edge of the table, thinks, What is cutting at Colin's heart to make him reveal his disillusion, his emptiness in words . . . ?

Maybe, though, Belinda merely composes a picture which casts doubt on the value or the truth of what Colin says.

Either of these would be a possibility. Perhaps she does not hear the words but only the tone, for now she says, 'My landlady grows hollyhocks in her Fulham garden.'

Also there is a butterfly on the window.

When Colin was much younger, an undergraduate at Cambridge, he used to chivy moorhens on the lawns that are called the Backs which fringe the river. He and a friend, a moody Irish peer, spent happy mornings driving the birds now here, now there; for some reason they never took off in flight but scuttled in alarm now here, now there. His friend had a German girl, whose suburban landlady was outraged when she heard of this sport. Believing that Colin and Dermot received government grants to enable them to pursue their studies she regarded the moorhen-driving as a waste of public money. Her anger was sport to them; they did not in fact receive grants but it would have been sport in any case. As it was it enlivened their picture of themselves as idle, rich and different.

In those days the moment was golden; it was grey at the edges now.

'When were you last in love?' Belinda asks.

'I suppose that question means you are,' he answers, pouring more wine.

She doesn't reply to this except by slipping from the table like a model when the photographer has put his camera away.

They cannot talk about love and surely both know the question should never have been asked.

In their family it is right, it is the done thing, to maintain silence on such matters and make jokes instead. Only at this moment when the evening is spread out against the sky and the butterfly is surely a moth, no jokes breathe life into their *pas-de-deux*.

But perhaps they can talk of others, and so Belinda says, 'Andrew's hair is going grey.'

And Colin replies, 'And yet our brother has chosen the life he leads. Better than baldness, I suppose. If Andrew went bald he would have to wear a wig.'

'Barber, barber, shave a pig, how many hairs to make a wig . . . do you remember?'

'No, I . . . suppose I never knew the answer.'

'Would you like a peach?' she says. 'I forgot, I brought some peaches. It's been hot in London, baskets of wonderful peaches outside the greengrocers at the corner, you could have thought yourself in Provence . . .'

He raises an eyebrow at that one.

The house broods, as it were, over the kitchen where Belinda senses its other life; for they are by no means alone there.

Upstairs, in the main bedroom, above the bow-fronted drawing-room, once perhaps the minister's study, lies Grace who is dying. Belinda's memories of Grace are all sharp. She sees Grace organizing picnics, peeling hard-boiled eggs, all she does is done with a sweet acerbity; the smoke of Turkish cigarettes continually arising from the saucer of her ever-present coffee cup. She likes to think that Grace's life has been one without regrets; the sharp pain of death accepted, experienced, never poisoning the memory. It may not have been like this at all, of course; which is something Belinda is ready to admit. Her Grace is Grace formed by her, but certainly not, she is certain, deformed by the act of her imagining. Grace has never appeared in *Who's Who*; an entry in such a book would be thin, for there has been nothing centrally public in her life. Her ridiculous husband, Grandpa Major, had been for years Conservative, or rather Unionist, Member of Parliament; Grace had taken tea on the terrace of the House in the spirit of the purest irony. In the Commons she liked Robert Boothby and Walter Elliott; she had been surprised into admiration of Churchill in 1940, but never succumbed to idolatry. It was perhaps strange judgement to find Churchill vulgar and Boothby, whose whisky breath and rich humorous boom Belinda recalled from childhood, not. Belinda is now accustomed to see Grace in sepia photographs which have actually never existed. Her Cordelia voice . . . the way in which her style of dress refused to defy old age . . . and she was, Belinda has always believed, faithful to her husband. Perhaps she disliked sex . . .

Certainly the case with her sister Annie, who, Belinda knows, will be sitting by a window, deploring the countryside and regretting the absence of a street where she could keep detailed watch on the comings and goings of others. When she considers Annie, Belinda is first amazed by the distance Grace has travelled and wishes she had some sense of social-historical perspective that could make sense of it. For Annie is, in Colin's phrase, '*echt* D C Thomson fodder'. There are grounds for thinking virgin Annie a maniac; her malice and her bursts of fury, where her tongue strikes out faster than ever serpent struck but with no certainty of aim, give ballast for such opinion. Colin indeed, who is her favourite among the great nephews and nieces, considers her certifiable;

lunatics seeing Aunt Annie at large write letters to their M.P.s, he put it. Annie hates sex; for a long time she has shuddered on seeing Belinda, which, Belinda reflects, might cause some to call her judgement in question. Annie is a dependent who bullies. On Grace's first stroke she abandoned Broughty Ferry and her semi-detached bungalow (close to a busy corner) and settled in the manse to run, perhaps redress, the life she has so long disapproved and envied. That at least is how Belinda sees it; for all she knows there may be those, in Broughty Ferry perhaps, who consider Annie a martyr. She has never worked, but she has organized the work of others.

Now, later, in bed, where Belinda lies straight, stretched-out flat on her flat belly, and cannot sleep, thoughts turn to the quarrels and dissensions between Grace and Annie; for coming home—and this has always been Belinda's nearest to home—coming home to a death is a time for excavation.

Grace and Annie quarrel about the peacock. Annie fears the peacock which sometimes runs at her with spear-like neck; even more though she dislikes it when it flaunts its tail. And yet the peacock could serve as a Calvinist text, if Belinda could remember verses of the Bible.

There is no doubt that Annie thinks she has won a life-long battle. Grace is stricken and she herself moves nimbly on busy feet, her nose twitching in inquisition.

Think of their dress. Belinda sees her grandmother in lace, her great-aunt in synthetic tweed. This may not be representationally accurate.

It is not quite black in the bedroom in the summer night. Beyond the window Belinda senses that the night is never still.

Annie admires Belinda's mother. Diana has got on; she is a woman of power. Belinda sees a Diana Annie does not know, the Diana who with a look and a backward gesture of her head summons a young man of uncertain accent from a girl's side. It is important he moves with chunky dynamism; that is all. There is no jealousy, could not be, for in fact Belinda finds her mother's young men unattractive. She dislikes their ambition. They are men determined to get on, who have discarded boyhood long ago, whatever naïveté they may in their souls retain. They never think about their souls; nothing deader than consciousness of soul in the world of women's magazines Diana dominates.

Diana dominates. Annie catches the power she sends out and basks; a basking shark, mouth slightly open. Grace, though, has a way of saying to Belinda 'your mother'; her irony illuminates and Belinda has long warmed in gratitude. What Grace has been to her has called her home . . .

Belinda knows her mother cannot come up till Grace is dead. Not because of the pressure of business; Diana takes a week, ten days, in St Tropez whenever she chooses, but death is another matter and she doesn't like it. She'll settle business afterwards though.

It is curious how Annie shudders at Belinda but not at her mother. Belinda moves her right leg softly to and fro and runs her hand under her flat belly, then stretches both hands out beyond her head so that her fingers touch the bed-head. She can hear Colin moving, a little uncertainly, up the stairs. He knocks something over, or drops it, and there is a muttered oath. Poor Colin. Belinda cannot think other than this, even though she knows Colin is waiting for Grace's death in hope. It is a question of the will; who gets the house? What else will Grace leave? How much? And to whom?

No doubt Annie expects the house, for life at least . . . being Annie she will resent it if that is all she gets, or rather how she gets it. She would like it outright . . . then she in her turn could play a will game . . . not that Grace does that.

Colin resumes his unsteady progress. The house will not save him; perhaps he needs a war. He is the sort of man whom 1914 rescued and 1915 killed. Nevertheless getting the house could check his descent. The door of his bedroom bangs and Belinda begins to drift towards sleep.

The morning mist droops on the rhododendrons. Belinda shivers as she pulls on jeans and a sweater thicker than she has worn in London for weeks. She descends the stair to the kitchen, which rests like a lair at the bottom of the silent house. All feels damp and clammy.

There is a banging of pots in the kitchen. It is Aunt Annie. Her busy step tittups.

'So you've arrived.'

'Last night.'

From old habit she leans over and kisses Annie's faded cheek. She avoids her lips. Aunt Annie, it comes back to her, has a wet kiss.

'How is she this morning? It was too late to see her when I arrived last night.'

'She's up and down. She feels sorry for herself, won't make an effort.'

'Does the doctor come every day?'

'Of course he does. Overdoes it if you ask me—his visits fret her. She thinks if he comes so often she must be dying.'

Belinda doesn't say Isn't she? Instead she asks after Annie's health.

'I get flushes. Nobody thinks there's ever anything the matter with me but if your grandmother sneezes . . .'

'You must have a lot on your hands . . .'

'And no thanks for it. How's your mummy?'

It is hard to think of Diana as Mummy.

'She's not easily fooled. She doesn't panic,' says Annie. 'And of course her job's responsible. I told Grace that. Diana, I said, has a lot of responsibility, she can't just lay it down.'

What can Belinda say to this? She could say, 'Responsibility, Christ! There are several reasons why dear Mummy as you call her won't come up and you wouldn't like to hear a single one of them. In the first place, she can't stand the idea of death. She's even more frightened of it than you are. It's something she can't control and ever since she got rid of my father, whom you never liked, she has been very careful, oh ever so careful, to keep everything in life under control. In the second place, she wants to go to St Tropez next weekend with her current chum, who, my dear Aunt Annie, is a Cockney yob of my age, working on the gossip column of

22

one of the gutter papers. He's also laying a slut in his office but dear Diana-always-in-control-of-everything doesn't realize this. I should think he's costing her a couple of thousand a year; but he flatters her.'

Belinda says none of this. Last night when she said it to Colin, his only comment was, 'I take it he's a J double O?'

'I've no idea.'

'I trust our mother is past breeding, I have no wish for half-brothers with big noses.'

'I don't think we've ever had any need to worry about half-brothers.'

'Indeed no, ought we to be grateful?'

So now Belinda makes herself some coffee.

She sits at the table, resisting the temptation to take the coffee to another room.

Annie says, 'And how's Andrew?'

When Belinda suddenly found herself alone, Annie with a sniff and her rapid inquisitive step having taken herself off, she knew it was time to go to see Grace, but couldn't and sat there on the high-backed chair, sensing the morning. The door to the yard was open. She could smell rain. You went to the cities to see life; it came to you in the country.

She was afraid she would find Grace diminished. In that case, for the first time in her life, she wouldn't know how to talk to her. Even as an adolescent, when she had all at once seemed all leg, and been held in apprehension by the fear that she would never have breasts, even then, she had talked to Grace with chamber music fluency. In itself cause for love.

'I think you must be Belinda.'

Voice with the rasp and burr of the North-East overlaid by education. She looked up to see a stranger perhaps a few years older than she, who had somehow made an inaudible descent to the kitchen and now stood regarding her with an expression she couldn't interpret.

'I was sent to look for you.'

'I'm sorry,' she said, idiotically.

'Don't apologize. We haven't actually met. I'm Patrick Craig.'

'Dr Craig?'

'That's right. Grace would like to see you, when it's convenient.'

'Oh how is she?'

She was aware of sounding fifteen, being gauche. She could always surprise strangers, who had heard of her, by displays of gaucheness.

Patrick Craig said, 'The correct answer is, I suppose, as well as can be expected.'

'That means there's no hope.'

'Miracles happen, but if they don't, it's only a question of time.'

'And you don't expect a miracle.'

'It's not, I suppose, by definition, something you can expect.'

She looked at him properly for the first time. He had an appearance of belonging. You might say, here's a good member of a good community.

'You like her, don't you?'

'Very much.'

'I've been sitting here, not wanting to go up.'

'Unnecessary. I think if you went immediately, actually, it would be better. She sleeps a lot.'

'Is that with a drug?'

'She wouldn't easily sleep without, and she is weak. She's very pleased you've come.'

Belinda's hand flew up to push back loose hair.

Patrick Craig said, 'Annie gets on her nerves, but you'll know that of course.'

Belinda nodded. 'It's good of you to come in search of me; sorry you've had to.'

As she went upstairs she realized that she had never really looked at his face, wouldn't be able to describe what he looked like. She hoped she would recognize him. Silly to imagine not.

She was glad she had met him before seeing Grace. He

gave her the medical authority to accept that she was dying.

And she could see she was. That was horrifying. She leant over and kissed her, like no other kiss she had ever given. She pressed Grace's hand, feeling the separate bones.

'I should have come sooner,' she said.

It was an admission that she knew how things were.

There was a silence.

What else could there be? Gallant small-talk? Describe her journey?

The silence meant acceptance. She had come to see her out. Till then . . .

'We can't really go out to dinner,' she said to Colin. It was two days after her arrival.

'Why not?'

'I don't want to anyway.'

'In the midst of death we are in life.'

She didn't in fact understand his determination, apart of course from its mulishness. Dinner parties—country dinner parties especially—weren't in Colin's line.

'What do you mean by that?'

He gave a little shrug, an irritating shrug. He couldn't be pretending either that Grace wasn't going to die or that her death wasn't important. So what did the shrug say? That death was old-fashioned? We have of course to pretend now that death is a solecism; something in rather bad taste. The notion of gathering for a death-bed, which was what they had actually done, was ridiculous. Worse than ridiculous, which it could only be considered by those who refused to think about it at all and preferred just to dismiss the idea. But it actually called far too much in question. It suggested that other scales of values might in reality operate. So, to avoid giving offence, you had to go out to dinner whenever you were asked. She could see Colin's line. But it was new for him to care about giving offence. He must deep down share something of the attitude, the distaste.

25

'I told Fiona you wouldn't like it,' he said, his voice lightening with the irony he reserved for mention of their younger sister (the one he had described as 'the successful one'). 'She said, "Belinda doesn't go in for that mawkish Victorian stuff. You have to go on living," she said. To put it my way again, in the midst of death we are in life; actually, I rather like that expression.'

'God, you're vile.'

'Anyway Fiona has had this dinner planned for weeks. Who knows, as she rightly implies, how long Grace will take. Charles II, one sometimes feels, wasn't in it when it comes to taking an unconscionable time a-dying . . .' He lit a cigarette. 'Fiona's a good wee modern,' he said.

'But really, don't you feel it's rather horrible?'

'Up to a point, but does it matter?'

What ought to happen when Colin makes remarks like this is a sudden eclipse of whatever light there is. And oddly when Belinda looked out of the window she saw that the heavy clouds were at last opening and big drops of rain falling.

'Why does Fiona want me?' Belinda said. 'I'd have thought she wouldn't. She can't want to show me off, she doesn't enjoy my company.'

'She wants you to see her in her glory.'

That was nonsense. The truth was simpler (as usual). Fiona was deeply conventional. The conventions said that a returned sister must be dined. No need for your actual fatted calf. Salmon mayonnaise from the deep-freeze would probably be the order of the day.

'Come off it,' she said, but found herself giggling.

'She went to Edinburgh and got a new dress from Jenners when she heard you were coming. She'll have had her hair done.'

'That's nothing. Fiona's been to the hairdresser's every week for the last—I can't remember when she left school. Every week since then anyway. It was one of the first things she despised in me that I never went to the hairdresser. Poor thing.'

'Who? Fiona? Pathetic yes, but not, I should have thought,

a worthy object of sympathy. Annie has enormous respect for her.'

'To win Aunt Annie's respect is hardly a talisman—or do I mean testament? She's really a Fascist, objectively looked at.'

'I didn't know you cared about Fascism, not I should have thought your style . . .'

Put like that, in Colin's mocking tones, again Belinda could only giggle. She was apolitical, thought it all silly and ineffably boring. Nevertheless, hysterical and hypocritical as were such manifestations of contemporary anti-Fascism as she had encountered, or as had forced themselves upon her, there was yet such a thing, at core, as Fascism. For her, to call someone a Fascist was a moral judgement. A Fascist was one who in the last resort would approve anything which seemed to protect his threatened interest. That was distasteful and inelegant; it was therefore an aesthetic judgement she made also.

There were moments when Belinda, surveying her family, could only say, 'What a set of rats we are, what a collection of insufferable attitudes.'

'All right,' she said to Colin, 'how can I stand out?'—but she could, if she wanted to—'how can I stand out?'—to stand out would be priggish, and who of any sensibility dares to be a prig, who can be a conscious prig?—let the word merely present itself and any action to be labelled priggish becomes immediately impossible—oh God, so . . . now . . . again . . . feeling a heel, she said, 'All right, how can I stand out?'

At that moment, when she was consenting as so often to something that shamed her, the telephone rang. It was Oswald, her ex-husband. Or rather it was Felicity, Oswald's secretary and—or so she had once believed, but now no longer cared—mistress, to say that Oswald would like to speak to her.

'Tell him to bugger off,' said Colin.

She agreed but said, 'Yes, of course, Felicity.'

Oswald said, 'What's the news?'

'What's it got to do with you?'

The trouble was, nothing she could say had ever managed to offend Oswald. His conceit was impervious.

'I don't believe that doctor's any good,' he said.

'Are you mad? What doctor? What on earth are you talking about?'

'I met Diana yesterday and she said Grace was only being treated by the local doctor. That's ridiculous. Local doctors are only G.P.s. They never know anything.'

'You've become a medical authority too now, have you?'

'Don't be silly. The man you want to get hold of is Stephen Machonie, I think that's his name, but you can check it. He's a consultant in Edinburgh. I was talking to Guy Pettigrew, just after I met Diana, and he assured me Machonie was the man for the case. If that's his name. Check it, Felicity, would you? How are you, Belinda?'

'Oh I'm fine.'

'I may be in Scotland next week. I'll come and see you.'

'Oswald, let me ask you something. Did you hear that we'd got a divorce?'

'What's that got to do with it?'

'I only wondered whether you knew, that's all . . .'

'Ask him,' Colin said, 'if he knows a good hairdresser . . .' She put her hand over the mouthpiece. 'Why?'

'Do him credit at Fiona's . . .'

'Nobody ever fails to do Oswald credit, didn't you know? Being connected to him means that they acquire merit. Anyway I'm not any longer, thank God, connected.'

'Then why don't you put down the receiver?'

And she did just that.

'Jumped many counters recently, your ex-husband?' asked Colin.

'You ought to know. Oswald made his definitive counter-jump years ago.'

'With his marriage, are you suggesting . . . ?'

'Not exactly . . .'

'Nevertheless one still detects the shadow of a counter, a

spectral counter perhaps. They seem to loom around him . . .'

The marriage had not been disastrous quite from the start. All the same, Belinda blushed when she considered how she had allowed it to happen. She liked to tell herself, I could never have been in love with Oswald . . . In love, in love, Colin would say, what you mean in love, is sex, that's all. It might be, but somehow that was even worse. To be romantically deceived was one thing, to have been lured by that heavy, big-buttocked body something rather worse. It suggested either a responsive vein of coarseness in herself or a lack of some kind. But could there be a lack that Oswald was capable of supplying?

Of all that she had ever done Belinda was most ashamed of her marriage.

But perhaps it had merely been more evidence of the weakness of her will. Oswald had said, you'll marry me, and that was that. Actually he'd never even put it as plainly. Marriage, like her first succumbing, had merely been so weightily assumed that there seemed nothing she could do.

Oswald, this was the joke, had been as wrong about her in his turn. He had been deceived by her manner into believing that Belinda would be a social asset. If he had investigated her past, how quickly the illusion would have been dispelled. The time for instance when she was working for that firm of publishers that he would certainly have described in his horrid jargon as 'prestigious'; certainly all the other girls on the editorial staff had been upper-class, county; that would have impressed Oswald, a frightful snob for all his meritocratic manner; unfortunately, as Belinda put it, 'the only people I got on with were the cleaning wifies. They were fine.' Not what Oswald would have wanted. His own manner to cleaning women, like his way with waiters, was appalling: vulgar, bullying and jocular.

Yet—and this was certainly part of the reason for it all—he had energy. It was perhaps inevitable that Colin's sister should be attracted towards energy, at least once. For some time too, he had been puzzling: she could never understand exactly what he did. 'Industrial Consultant' was quite meaningless, and when he said, 'you could call me a social psychiatrist' she wasn't any the wiser. It was anyway ridiculous to suppose that Belinda could ever call anyone a social psychiatrist.

She had early in their marriage been dismayed by the effeminacy of his taste. It was at once prissy and tarty; taste formed by studying the glossies. And therefore vulgar.

They moved into Oswald's flat in Cornwall Gardens. He had done a lot of work on it and saw no reason to move. Belinda doubted if any marriage could survive on that basis; a house had either to be ancestral or the woman's creation. As it was she couldn't even change the apricot and mauve of the bathroom or remove the tasselled light-shade in the hall.

All that she stood up to a point. It wasn't even the Scandinavian kitchen that drove her out. It was Oswald's maddening good temper and his conversation. Good temper wasn't quite right. He was frequently testy and snappish. What he wouldn't do was quarrel. Whenever she tried he would put himself in her place and tell her how she saw it; then he would talk of the broader issues. Eventually Belinda wanted to throw things when she heard these ghastly words. Once she did; a beer tankard. It missed.

At least there had been no children. To have had a child of Oswald's would have been a permanent humiliation. At first she had resented Oswald's reluctance to start a family; a baby would displace him. Later she had been grateful. Later hadn't been long in coming.

Now she said to Colin, 'We've neither of us been much good at marriage, have we?'

Colin said, 'Well, it's pretty well known I'm useless. Can't expect quality from anyone prepared to marry me, but Julie, though a little bitch, isn't a cad and counter-jumper.'

'In the mood for judgements are you?'

'Heavens no, merely observing.'

'You must be the last man left alive who can talk of cads.'

'Shouldn't think so.'

30

Belinda was annoyed to find herself nervous. You shouldn't be nervous before going to dinner at your sister's; your little sister's.

The telephone rang. She waited for Colin to answer it. In vain. It was Martin.

'Thought I'd let you know that Jill and I will be leaving in five minutes. So we'll be with you in twenty. Give you a chance to be ready.'

Nevertheless she wasn't of course and when she eventually came downstairs she could see Jill was angry. Colin had given Martin a drink. Presumably Jill had refused the one she certainly didn't have.

Belinda nodded to her, sat on the arm of a sofa and took the gin-and-tonic Colin had ready.

'We ought to be off,' said Jill, 'we're already late.'

'It's not my habit,' said Colin, 'to worry about punctuality.'

He sipped his gin.

'Besides,' he added, 'it's good for Fiona to have to wait.'

Belinda took a good look at Jill. She had controlled her tendency to run to fat. That must have taken determination. Was she happier as a result? Martin looked even worse than the first evening.

'Who'll be there?' Belinda asked.

'The usual crowd,' Colin said. 'Plus such nobs as Fiona has managed to nobble. She's developing delusions of grandeur, our wee sister.'

'I don't know why you always sneer at Fiona,' said Jill.

'No,' said Colin, 'I suppose not. I hope it will be a proper dinner. At one time Fiona had a distressing fondness for what she called fork suppers.'

'Fork suppers, how distressing!' said Belinda, playing up, stressing 'how'.

'I hope I've cured her of it,' Colin said, 'I told her I preferred fish ones.'

'Did she get it?'

'Who can tell.'

And Martin still hadn't spoken.

Jill began to talk quickly, as it were nervously, about local affairs, no one listening . . .

'Of course,' she said, running down, 'you'll have heard that we've all become politicians. For my part . . .'

'Time to go,' said Martin.

Without waiting for any response he picked up the shooting-jacket he had earlier thrown over the back of a chair and made for the door. He didn't look round to see if they were following. In certain circumstances it could have seemed a blithe display of confidence. To Belinda it looked as if he was leading a probably forlorn hope, and didn't care whether the men came over the trench after him or not.

They met Annie in the hall. She was arranging flowers, badly; not something she often did, but there aren't many pieces of work that can be done in the hall of a house in the country on a summer evening.

'Revelling?' she said as they passed, and sniffed, not to smell her flowers. Jill, though, stopped to talk. She and Annie respected each other.

Pink streaks lit the sky between the dark trees and a heavy cloud. The dew was already dampening the grass. The peacock came rushing at them, neck outstretched and pecking angrily. They were able to ignore it and drive away.

Fiona was what every girl should wish to be. Wife, mother, with the sort of looks other girls admire, clothes eminently suitable for one couldn't quite tell what—lunching in smart department stores perhaps—intelligent but not intellectual, correct. The adjective 'groomed' attached itself to her, wholly admirable product of the Public School system; what a Prefect and Captain of Hockey she had been; how the thirteen-year-olds, adoring her, had blushed when she addressed them. She had married at twenty-four, after five years as secretary to a most successful architect. She had two children, a blonde girl and a red-headed boy; she called them 'lambs'. As indeed they were. Her husband had not yet been unfaithful; she had never been tempted into adultery, which she considered dirty. She knew a lot about country houses and did voluntary work for a society pledged to defend rural parish churches. She couldn't understand people who chose to live in the city; they were morally suspect, though might be acquitted if they shot or fished or skied at week-ends.

She kissed Belinda, because you kissed your sister.

'What a lovely dress,' she said.

'I do like your hair,' she said to Jill.

'It's just a small party, all old friends,' she said to Martin.

'I asked Patrick Craig,' she said to Colin. 'Do you think he's all right for Grace?'

'Have you met him?' she said to Belinda. 'He's a good doctor but he needs looking after. Remind me to tell you about his wife.'

There were perhaps a dozen people in the room and though they might all be old friends of Martin, Belinda discovered that she recognized none. That measured the distance her life had moved, that she could come to what she thought of as her home country and recognize nobody at her sister's house. For a moment she felt an emptiness, a sadness as of a loch-side when the sun has sunk behind the hills; then dismissed it from her mind as a piece of sentimental insincerity. But to dismiss something from your mind is not to lighten your spirit; she was still conscious of a vacancy. She could even sense a jealousy of Fiona. It was something to have accepted the conditions of your existence so fully. She had been educated to regard such unquestioning acceptance as a weakness; she couldn't be sure it wasn't in fact a strength. She watched Fiona talk, head tilted, feet planted apart; a natural sturdiness lay behind every gesture. She was talking to a dark-haired man with a lined, bored face and obviously telling him what was what. Then she laughed but he didn't respond. She pouted slightly and the strength and boredom both slipped from his expression; he was only someone who'd already perhaps had too much gin.

A voice behind her said, 'I was hoping you'd decide to come. That was how Fiona got me here, promising you'd come . . .'

She turned round to see the Doctor.

'How nice of you to say that . . . not that I believe you, but go on if you like . . .'

'You were looking a bit lost . . .'

'How I was feeling . . . to be somewhere where you ought to be and feel you don't belong, it's odd. Grace was sleeping when we left.'

'She'll sleep a lot just now . . . then less or with more medication . . . I'm really a nurse, not a doctor for her.'

'Do you know someone called Machonie?'

'Edinburgh?'

She had spoken on impulse; it had to be carried forward.

'Is he any good? My ex-husband who's an idiot thinks we should consult him.'

'He's very good. There's nothing he could do though. I knew you had an ex-husband. I'm surprised he's an idiot . . .'

'I was misinformed, you see. I thought he wasn't . . .'

'We all make mistakes . . .'

They went through to the dining-room, Fiona getting them all to move without fuss. She should have been a general; on the Staff anyway. Belinda noticed Colin turn back, a deserter. He moved to the drink table to re-fill the gin glass which he now carried through.

Belinda found herself placed beside Fiona's husband, Gavin. This place of honour (or at least respect) would have been dismaying if Patrick Craig hadn't been put on her other side. And that, though agreeable, stirred a little irritation. Fiona had never been distinguished for her tact; successful school prefects aren't, too full of moral rectitude to require tact also.

Gavin was embarrassed. He had admired Oswald. Belinda had once heard him describe Oswald as 'astonishing fellow, awfully persuasive you know, the sort of chap who deserves encouragement'—there was nothing that Oswald had ever needed less. Gavin began to talk about politics to the thin woman on his left. 'They're crazy of course,' she heard him say; 'I'm as good a Scot as anyone, actually entitled to the tartan I wear, which is more than can be said . . . say nothing of my regimental one . . . but the fact of the matter is we couldn't last five years on our own. What you've got to look at is the sort of chaps who would run the country . . . take my word for it, Betty, they wouldn't be decent fellows like you and me . . .'

'Who wants to be ruled by Glasgow?' snapped Betty, whoever she was. She asked the question as if she were suddenly putting a point that had just occurred to her.

'I've always rather liked Glasgow,' Belinda said, 'better than Edinburgh anyway . . .' The look Betty gave her should have been directed through a lorgnette.

'How's the fishing, Gavin?' she said.

'God knows what they'd do with that, that's what I'd like to know. When the oil's gone what are we to live on? Whisky?'

'Some of us already do,' said Colin.

'I don't know what you're up to, Martin,' said Betty, 'trying to get rid of Mansie Niven. He talks more sense than any other Scottish Member.'

'Well,' said Martin, 'it doesn't look as though we're going to succeed. But I'll tell you this, I'd as soon vote for a bullfrog myself . . .'

Salmon mayonnaise succeeded the soup; the hock was inferior. Gavin had always bought his drink with regard to price rather than value, a habit Belinda had no doubt Fiona approved. Wine brought out the Puritan in her.

'I used to know Mansie,' she said to Patrick Craig. 'I mean, I used to meet him at dances. He wore a lace jabot.'

'He still does.'

'How frightful; I mean he's older than I am, he must be nearly forty. There's something depressing in a middle-aged man taking that sort of style . . . I'm awfully bad at explaining. I mean I like men to take trouble over what they wear only if it's the right sort of trouble; and Mansie's isn't. He's got a wet kiss too—like Annie's actually . . .'

'That's an interesting piece of information. You won't be surprised that it's new to me.'

'It was at a Hunt Ball he kissed me. I didn't enjoy it . . .'

'Good . . .'

35

'What I object to,' said the dark-haired man Fiona had been talking to, 'is that it's all a bloody pointless diversion. There's only one problem facing Western Civilization and that's how to maintain some sort of hierarchy. Everything else is guff . . .'

But that was going too far. Western Civilization might pass as an expression; just. Hierarchy wouldn't do. No one took him up on it. Belinda wondered who he was. A few years ago, Colin would have plunged in on that one. His fingers now played round the stem of his empty wine-glass. He'd finished the gin also, she noticed.

'Hierarchy' had given the conversation a momentary stop. Gavin started to tell Betty about problems he was having with his new tourist development . . . a small village of holiday chalets . . .

'They steal the sheets from off the bed . . .'

'You should chain them to it,' said Colin. 'The tourists, not the sheets . . .'

'They bring their children of course and they draw on the walls. I'm having them sprayed . . .'

Patrick Craig's attention had been claimed by the woman on his right. Belinda, paying no attention to Gavin, tried to work out who was who. The woman Betty must be single—like me, she thought, divorced. She's bitter though. Stupider, I hope to God. Next to Betty was Martin, then a boy, by far the youngest member of the party, whom she'd heard addressed as Kenneth. It came to her that he must be Gavin's younger brother. He'd been at Prep School at the time of the wedding where he had been a page, a very decorative page she remembered. Now he seemed all arms and legs, skin and bone. Belinda could easily grip his thin wrist between thumb and forefinger, almost as he held his wine-glass. He had been sitting in silence. Now he looked up. Belinda saw dark-blue eyes. He looked away and blushed. There was no one for him to talk to. Martin stared moodily or deadly into space, while on his other side Jill devoted her attention to the dark-haired man Belinda had decided must be a colonel; perhaps not, hierarchy suggested an academic.

He in his turn continued to talk to Fiona, leaving Jill hanging as it were on their conversation. Whoever he was, he had more energy than anyone else there. He was the evening's big gun, the real reason for the dinner. Opposite him, on Fiona's left, was a monstrously fat, frigid woman. Belinda remembered her of old, a Mrs Rutherford. Husband dead. Self-inflicted wound. 'The old gun-cleaning lark,' as Colin put it. 'Who shall blame him? Marriage to Margot is a hero's role and he was no hero. Not that I don't adore her. She's all right. Only formidable.' The last word pronounced in the French manner. Then Colin; listening to her. Then the woman who had abstracted Patrick Craig. Someone's wife, she supposed.

There was a certain nastiness in the air, not to be elucidated till later.

'Do you think Fiona meant it?' Belinda was to ask.

'Could you get such a party together by accident?' said Colin. 'That would take talents of disorganization denied our prudent wee sister . . . no, no, ducky, get a girl ensconced in a successful dead marriage like Fiona and watch her make the shit fly . . .'

It didn't though strike Belinda as deliberate while it was happening. On the contrary she felt sorry for Fiona. Someone so conventional must feel ill-at-ease when a party she was giving threatened to break up in discord; when knives could be seen to flash.

Betty said, 'What's happened is that nobody has any standards in this country any more. Bloody socialism. You know, I was in Edinburgh last week and just turning into Jenners when I heard a man behind me in the street say to his wife, "What the hell do you expect, nobody in this bloody country wants to do anything nowadays", common flat Midland voice he had. Ten years ago I'd have turned round and told him to keep his opinions to himself. Not bloody likely now. I mean to say, when even someone like that can see what's wrong, the rot's galloping isn't it . . . ?'

'But,' said the dark-haired man, 'it's necessary, isn't it, to enquire into the causes . . .'

37

'Causes are obvious, Colonel,' snapped Betty.

'Well,' said the woman next to Patrick Craig, 'I'll tell you something, I'm jolly glad to be going back to South Africa next week, there are still some standards of behaviour there . . .'

'Good for you, Grizel,' said Gavin; 'wish Father hadn't sold his estate in Natal, never understood what possessed him . . .'

Martin looked over at Belinda. He said, 'The trouble is, what would any of you have to offer instead of what we've got; that's surely a question we've got to answer . . . Colonel there stands for hierarchy and I respect that, but how's it to be determined . . . ?'

'Respect.'

'Standards.'

'Decency.'

'A touch of the whip if you ask me . . .'

'Or the sjambok, Grizel . . .'

'I don't see, Martin, how you can honestly shrink from what's tough if you are defending what you believe to be good, just because a lot of commies and left-wing pansies . . .'

Patrick Craig said, 'Of course I'm only a doctor and there's a convention growing up that we are some sort of technicians who shouldn't allow ourselves the luxury of political opinions, but I don't, if you'll allow me to say so, really see in what way things are supposed to be so bloody awful . . .'

'Well if you won't you can't . . .'

Belinda was bleary-bored; whenever people started to talk like this, and the opinions were nothing, it was the tone of voice—Oswald's parties had always been dominated by people anxious to discuss these broader issues which never led anywhere, which quickened nothing—whenever, whenever, then Belinda . . .

looked out of the window,

gazed into the paintings on the other wall (bewigged eighteenth-century figures, ancestors or pseudo-ancestors of Gavin),

summoned up the past,

38

imagined love,
and now saw death.

Grace was weaker every day . . .

'I mean,' said Patrick Craig, 'whether you like it or not,
and it's pretty clear that most people here tonight don't, the
fact remains that life today for the majority, the vast majority
of people in this country, is a damn sight better than it's
ever been . . .'

'But who pays for it . . . ?'

'Bollocks, old boy,' said Gavin, 'simply bollocks.'

The boy, Kenneth, had given up all pretence of listening.
He was playing with his fork, crumbling bread, twisting his
wine-glass, gazing into the night, his long upper lip drooping
in boredom . . .

'Thing is,' said Grizel, 'you've all gone soft here . . .'

Soft . . . velvet . . . the softness of lips, roses, flesh, cushions,
beds . . .

Colin gestured to the manservant. 'Greig,' he said, 'my
glass is empty, hadn't you noticed?'

Belinda sensed Greig's glance at Fiona only when she
caught her sister's barely perceptible nod . . .

'You're afraid of people who know what they want and
take it, and in fact you're absolutely determined that energy
should never be rewarded. You're all wet . . .'

'Oh, well.'

But what is this energy in which I am so deficient . . .
Belinda wondered . . . or rather why am I? Is it a matter of
seeing both sides of a question and so finding nothing worth
doing . . . even when I want to; I so often don't, but I
wouldn't call myself lazy.

She looked through the candles of the candelabra again at
Kenneth, at the indistinct corners of his mouth and the long
fine fingers playing with the stem of the glass.

Fiona rapped on the table. She spoke in her clear voice of
a thousand meetings. She said, 'I don't want to make a
speech. That's not at all what I intend to do. Still there are a
couple of things I want to say. First, it's jolly nice to see
Belinda here home again. I won't say we've never had rows,

39

what sisters haven't, outside a nunnery maybe, but at least we have always been able to respect each other . . .'

Is Fiona drunk . . . oh no . . . Belinda's thoughts go into a tumbling spin.

'Things haven't gone as well for her as they might have, while I've been jolly lucky, but I'm sure that some of you other girls who've been through difficult times will join with me in wishing that things go better in future, whether patching up the past or making a new start . . .'

Belinda tried to keep her gaze down.

'That's the first thing,' said Fiona, 'and we'd have had a dinner even if it had only been that, but I wanted you all, family and close friends to have a proper chance of meeting Colonel Morgan. I don't mind telling you, that we, that is, Gavin and myself, have been more impressed by Colonel Morgan than by anyone we've met in ages; I'm hoping I don't embarrass you too much, Gerald, by saying so. We're all concerned with public affairs now, and I'm sure I'm right in saying that we all of us, or almost all, recognize that we're in a crisis situation right now. It's my view and Gavin's too that we've got to listen to Gerald Morgan about this. It seems to us that he is someone who can speak with that authority we are all inwardly longing for. That's one reason why I've asked him here tonight, and I've taken the liberty of asking him if he will say a few words to us all. So, after dinner, we'll move through to the drawing-room for coffee and then Gerald Morgan will let us have the crisis situation and the way out as he sees it. There are some others coming in to hear him.

'Shall we,' Fiona gathered her troops with her assurance of a thousand meetings, giving, as Colin put it, her well-known imitation of the girl voted most likely to succeed by the sophomores of Bryn Mawr, 'go through?'

There ought to have been music . . .

The few more people were quite a few, not all dinable. The variety was itself evidence of Fiona's development. You wouldn't have found grocers and farmers who were only farmers (their fathers perhaps having been mainly tenants)

40

in her drawing-room a year or two ago. For the first time Belinda was curious. She said to Patrick Craig, 'What the hell is all this about? I don't at all begin to understand what is happening, but it hasn't altogether a pleasant feel.'

'Perhaps you've been insulated in London. Less and less that happens has.'

'It's not just this SNP business then?'

'Oh no, that's . . . what shall I say . . . incidental. A symptom rather than a cause. What do you smell in the air?'

'Roses of course, but something animal too . . .'

'Ever read Kipling . . . ?'

'Of course, who hasn't, but not for a long time . . . I loved *The Jungle Book* and even more *Kim* . . .'

'Well, it is fear, little brother, it is fear . . .'

Belinda looked up at him, her head at a slight angle. He had a face that convinced her. Some experience there; Oswald's face had begun to worry her soon after marriage, so unlined, so baby-skinned, not a real face at all. There was humour in the lines of Patrick Craig's too, absent of course from Oswald's. If only she felt . . . but she didn't. She hadn't of course with Oswald either; sheer induced dissimulation . . . What she couldn't simulate was the real *coup de foudre* that made an ass of you . . .

'This colonel,' she said, 'who is he . . . ?'

'Gerald Morgan; he bought Balholvie earlier this year, he's lived abroad, most recently in Rhodesia . . .'

'And got out . . .'

'Not I should think because of political differences, quite the reverse, but he's got a great sense of reality . . . look, you'll hear what he's like . . . I hear you used to fish. Come out with me one day next week, will you? I generally take Wednesday afternoon off . . .'

'I'd love to, it's years since . . .'

'That's fixed then, I've a rod you can use, the ones at Grace's are all past their best; greenhearts, the sap's mostly gone . . .'

'The sap's mostly gone, I know just how they feel . . . Greenhearts.'

'You shouldn't moan,' he said, 'it shouldn't really be your style . . .'

And then someone she didn't know claimed his attention, taking his sleeve and pulling him aside. She found she didn't resent what he had said, even though it was true. That was strange enough . . .

Fiona was calling them to order, reminding them of what was in store. Belinda looked over at Morgan. There was something impressive about the man, she supposed—but only if you had already decided he was going to impress you. She knew at once that she didn't want to hear what he was going to say, not just because she wasn't going to agree with it, there might be plenty that she would in fact agree with, but because of the manner. She didn't either like this cross between a conspiracy, a revivalist meeting and something she didn't immediately identify.

He was going to show a film or slides; someone was pinning a white sheet to the wall to serve as a screen.

That, of course, was it. Belinda slipped out of the french window.

There was dew on the grass and she was only wearing slippers. She didn't mind. The air was scented with honeysuckle and roses and it was soft and almost palpable. She breathed in deeply and walked under the shadow of an elm tree, where the moonlight fell in patterns. Hadn't there been a swing there when Gavin was a child . . . ?

She spoke aloud,

'Lovely are the curves of the white owl sweeping
Wavy in the dusk lit by one large star . . .'

But it was later than dusk, the moon was up and the owl nowhere . . . she felt the pain of childhood and the sweetness of the nineteenth century and she walked down the moss path of the yew alley.

At the bottom of the alley there was a figure alone, leaning over the wicket-gate. She hesitated, wondering who, like herself, had fled the hall. The night was not quite silent, she had become aware of myriads of soundlets. There was sweetness in all of them. And then the owl cried and, as she approached

the gate with silent, moss-deadened steps, it flew wings out-
spread across the field beyond. She coughed, very lightly, to
draw attention. The figure uncoiled from the gate. It was
Kenneth.

'You funked it too,' she said . . .

He nodded.

'I don't expect you . . .' she began . . .

'Why not,' he said, 'I wasn't such a baby . . .'

'You don't know what I was going to say.'

'Oh yes I do. Cleverer of you to recognize me, I've changed
more than you . . .'

'I worked it out that you must be Kenneth . . . I mean, you
are Kenneth aren't you . . . ?'

'So they tell me; I don't always feel it, not Kenneth Leslie
that is . . .'

'Who then . . . ?'

'Something out of nature . . .'

'I was thinking of Meredith as I came down the path.
"Love in the Valley", I think . . . "Lovely are the curves of
the white owl sweeping, wavy in the dusk lit by one large
star", and then it flew across the field . . .'

'Perfect timing, perhaps it means something . . .'

'When you say out of nature . . . ?'

'Obvious isn't it,' he said, 'I lean over gates and gaze at
owls in a vain attempt to re-establish contact . . .'

She sat down on the step of the stile beside the gate.

'I'm sorry about your grandmother,' he said.

'So am I. It's nice of you though.'

There was a silence but not an empty one.

'You looked very bored at dinner,' Belinda said at last.

'So did you.'

'Oh you noticed . . .'

'I looked at you a bit, I've been here being bored all summer, so I'm a good deal unluckier than you; that man Morgan's not exactly boring, he's creepy. I couldn't stand hearing
him again. Do you know his line?'

Belinda shook her head darkly.

'You look like a pony when you do that.'

'Thanks, thanks a lot.'

'Just for a moment . . . well you heard what it said about hierarchy. That silenced 'em of course, having more than two syllables—and that's one too many for Gavin—but the thing is, he really believes in it. Hierarchy, I mean, it's purely Fascist . . .'

'Oh God . . .'

'What do you mean, oh God . . . ?'

'It's so easy to say Fascist, I do myself, but people of our generation, not that I am your generation, I suppose, really shouldn't. I'm not political but to call something Fascist is to avoid having to think about it.'

'Well I don't want to think about his bloody hierarchy, it's obscene.'

'I expect you're right . . .'

'People aren't arranged in rungs according to birth, colour and so on. Not that I believe in equality, that's bloody silly too.'

'Let's talk about something else . . .'

'O.K.,' said Kenneth, 'there's something about the atmosphere here recently that has one talking in this absurd way . . .'

'Are you at University?'

'No, and I'm not sure I want to either. I'm supposed to be going in the autumn.'

'Why don't you want to?'

'Oh because everybody's so boring, telling me I'll always regret it if I don't.'

'Well, of course, that's a good reason but what's the first one? That must logically be secondary . . .'

'How do you work that out . . . ?'

'Nobody would say that if you hadn't first raised the possibility of not going . . .'

'*Touché.*'

'You didn't think I could argue like that, work things out all the way from A to B.'

'Hadn't occurred to me . . .'

'Well maybe it will now, don't underrate me . . .'

44

It was out of control. Belinda realized it even while it was happening, like being on a bicycle going downhill; you could steer into the ditch, but that was the only alternative to carrying on, for—no doubt about it—the brakes weren't working.

'Anyway,' she said, 'which one is it supposed to be?'

'Cambridge, Trinity . . .'

'Nothing wrong with that, I'd say . . . except I know what it is: you've taken Colin as a dreadful warning . . . I'm not sure though that even Trinity still breeds them like Colin . . . Magdalen, perhaps.'

'It's simpler than that, I just don't think I can stand any of it. Look, I'm sorry to inflict this on you . . .'

'Don't be silly, why shouldn't you say what you think; I don't care . . .'

Not about that, not about that . . . but this was Meredith crossed with Piaf—love in a valley in a café chansonnier. She drew the jersey she had picked up more firmly about her. A long way off she could hear the drone of an aeroplane engine. Grace's life was ebbing away, just as the sea withdrew from the sands; and her mother was twining with her young lout. The fatigue of the north and of the flesh.

Kenneth's slimness seemed a virtue; so she admired him. How could she fail to when she compared this with big-buttocked Oswald? And she shuddered with shame.

She said to herself: how pleasant it would be to kiss him, to be kissed by him.

She began to hope.

Love was born.

All this ran at once through Belinda's mind:

To love is to have the pleasure of seeing, touching, feeling in every way and experiencing with all the senses, as close as possible, someone lovable, who is prepared to love.

What was odd was that Belinda was aware that this was happening. She wanted to stretch out her hand, touch Kenneth's cheek, trace the line of his lips with her forefinger, feel him take it gently and cat-like in his teeth. It seemed impossible he wouldn't want to bite it, but gently.

45

A silence of expectation hung between them; only Belinda had that moment of absolute chilling doubt. Was the expectation all on her side?

Gerald Morgan flickered his hand and Fiona put a glass of water in it. He sipped, looking over the glass's rim at the audience.

'I'm going to sock it to you,' he said.

'Why are we all tired of politics, or put it another way, why are we disillusioned? It's not just that the politicians are liars. Politicians have always been liars and yet we used to be able to respect them. I'll tell you why. The old lies were merely deception. The politician wanted something and told a lie to get it. He knew it was a lie. We've got something different today. The whole damn thing is false, because it's based on a radically mistaken view of human nature. That's all.

'The nonsense goes like this. Men are naturally good. Unless you believe that, democracy makes no sense. It's rooted in that assumption. Rooted in this cock-eyed notion that men are naturally good. That's not my experience. I think they're by and large rotten. I'm not a religious man and I'll bet there aren't many here, so I'm not going to elaborate the doctrine of original sin, though I could, I could. And I'm not going to give you a philosophical discourse, though I could—I've Hobbes and Machiavelli at my finger-tips. I'm going to do something simpler. I'm going to ask you to look at yourselves and your neighbours. And what do you find—a lot of selfish, greedy, mischievous little animals. And yet you don't steal, you don't rape, you don't murder, you behave yourselves. Why?

'I'll tell you. Because you've had instilled in you, by your education, a certain discipline, certain standards. You've learned what it is permissible to do. Most of you have learned it so well that you can't even admit, because you don't know, what you would really like to do. And that's as it should be, if we are to have civilization.

'And how have you learned it? I'll tell you.

'In part by example, in part by exhortation, in part by fear.

46

'Fear.

'Most of us were beaten at school. It was good for us, not for the mucky sort of reason lefties would put forward that in some perverted way we enjoyed it, or it satisfied us. That's all balls. It was good for us, because it taught us that there were things it was safer not to do. It instilled social discipline, through the backside.

'That's what's missing. We've gone soft. Men are naturally good, naturally reasonable—it's all balls and deep down we know it. So it's time we said it. Men are mischievous and ignorant little brutes who will make a hash of what they undertake and a hell of this world if they are not . . .'

He went on like this for some time and when he stopped there was enthusiastic applause.

'Will they have missed us?' Belinda said, 'I'm sure Fiona will have noticed we're not there . . .'

'Oh Fiona. Your sister and my brother are well-matched. Though Gavin's stupider . . . look there's the owl coming back . . .'

Belinda put her hand on his sleeve, not on his cheek. She didn't speak. They watched the owl disappear into the trees and then turned and made their way back to the house.

'Promise you'll come over to see us,' Belinda said, 'it'll give you something to do . . .'

She wouldn't use Grace as an argument and fortunately it was unnecessary. Kenneth easily agreed; he wasn't even deterred by what she had said, that it would give him something to do.

She sat by her bedroom window still listening to the summer night. Sometimes she saw the black trees outlined softly against the sky that would never be quite dark. Or she abstracted herself and saw a fountain, the most delicious *in urbe et orbe* where in the soft evening the boys with the tortoises and dolphins gleamed watery-green, enchanting as Illyria. A Count Mattei had had it placed in what was now the Piazza

47

Mattei outside his palazzo as a wedding anniversary present for his wife. She had opened the bedroom shutters in the pink morning and, *eccoci!* And Belinda had seen it in the same way, years ago, her first morning in Rome, though the apartment she was staying in was on the other side of the Piazza.

It was what she thought of first if anyone said the word 'Renaissance'.

And she looked again across the darkened room at the engraving which hung above the wash-stand. No doubt at all, garlands of acanthus were becoming small neat, fine Classical heads . . .

She heard a step. The door opened, without any preliminary knock, and Colin entered. He had a bottle of whisky and two glasses.

'Symbiotically I knew you would not be asleep,' he said. 'I thought a spot of the famous *Lagopus Scoticus* might not come amiss. Calm the night's trembles and alert the morning's. *Ça va?*'

'Well enough.'

Colin was in a condition of drunkenness she recognized as perfect, though it was not one she ever achieved herself. He was in control, would do nothing untoward, yet contrived to be wholly detached from ordinary rules of existence. Everything he did or said would be arbitrary, making sense only within the logic of his turning wheel.

'Always,' said Colin, 'returning from such evenings I find myself insistently asking the question "are such people in any sense real?" Can they be said "truly to exist". One doubts it. Yet, of course, there are the alarming alternatives: a) yes they do exist and what's more I appear to them as they to me; b) they don't exist any more than the voices that chatter, chatter on the third and fourth day of abstinence, only these ones are doing it now, all the time. You must admit it's worrying, ducky.'

Colin could go on in this vein (which no doubt had some significance for him) endlessly. She couldn't stand it, though she took the half-tumbler of whisky he had poured out for her and put some water into it.

'I was a bit baffled by the whole evening,' she said.

'Not entirely surprising.'

'What's all this political mania?' Belinda said, 'I've never known anything like it here before, hardly even anywhere . . .'

Colin poured himself another half-tumbler of whisky and said nothing.

'Patrick Craig said it was fear,' said Belinda. 'Do you believe that?'

'Well, it's certainly not idealism, that's for sure.'

'It makes me wonder, this nervousness; we've been very lucky, haven't we, all our lives, being able to take politics for granted. Almost Bloomsbury it's been. After all, any political system that can incorporate Grandpa Major as one of the legislators is dedicated to the proposition that only the private life is real.'

'Politics can be an escape from the reality of the private life. Martin's private life is real enough. He just doesn't happen to like it. It's not an escape I've ever felt tempted to indulge in, but though thousands wouldn't believe it, *sorella mia*, there's nothing wrong with my private life, nothing that cutting my bank manager's throat wouldn't correct . . .'

'That might be interpreted as a dangerously revolutionary attitude.'

'The Catiline Conspiracy—absolute aim, the cancellation of debt; Catiline I've always found to be a guy after my own heart.'

Colin's heart . . . it is not an organ that Belinda easily believes in. And yet she knows she loves him and she feels he has affection for her—at any rate he would rather be with her than with anyone else. When they were younger . . . well, when they were younger, life spread out before them like a great African plain. You emerged from the cosy valley of childhood and stood on a ridge, under chestnut trees, seeing the valley widen beyond, descending to this plain of infinite possibility; in the distance you could discern the sea, a blue sheen lit by a summer sun. It was hard to see how you could lose your way on such a plain. Yet here was Colin entangled

49

in briars in an obscure wood, wild, rough and stubborn. She could not tell how he had found himself there; it was as if his departure from the true way had been with sleep-walking gait. And she herself . . .

The open window made the room cold. A slight breeze disturbed the light shade, round which the moths yet flickered.

Colin's marriage . . . Julie had been delightful. Belinda had always from the first day found her good value. Which was something, considering her prejudice against actresses. Colin had made her laugh. That was his strength.

Their first meeting was ludicrous. Colin, very drunk, had fallen on her in bed, as he climbed, homing, through the wrong open window. Julie had at once accepted his courteous explanation.

'I was aiming for my sister's window. I seem to have blundered.'

'That's all right,' she said, 'feel free.'

It was the time when girls were for the first time ever able to say, 'feel free' without bravado or affectation.

'Perhaps,' he said, producing a half of Glen Grant, 'you'd like a drink. I intended it for my sister, but, as the Frogs say, *les absents ont toujours tort* and consequently get omitted when the drinks are ordered. Got a toothmug?'

Julie had obliged and sat up in bed, pulling her legs under her.

'Do you do this often?'

'Now and again, now and again, when the spirit moves me . . .'

'Fall on strange beds, I mean, strange girls' beds at that . . .'

'Better surely than . . .'

'Strange boys, I'm glad to hear it.'

She hugged her knees, a long way naked under her shortie nightdress. Her lips formed themselves in a kissing pout. Colin didn't seem immediately to notice. She waited . . .

'It's funny,' she said, recounting it to Belinda, as she often did in time to come, 'I'm not really a tart.' (Belinda didn't believe her, but said nothing.) 'I was just so provoked because he seemed to concentrate on the whisky and conversation, exactly as if it was something we'd left off half an hour before. And I felt so tarty.'

At that moment the door bell rang and was immediately succeeded by loud banging.

'What on earth . . . ?'

'Who can tell . . . ?'

She had slipped on a dressing-gown and gone to the door. Two London bobbies stood there, one quite unnecessarily flashing a torch.

'You been disturbed, miss?'

'Well, you might say you are, disturbing me . . .'

'Less of that, miss, we had a report. Someone climbing through a window. Informant said it looked like yours. Thought it might be a burglar, she did.'

'Well well,' said Julie, feeling mischievous, 'fancy that. I'll tell you what it is. She wants to get me out of the flats.'

'Who does?'

'Your informant.'

'Does she now . . . ?'

'Loose living, that's what she accuses me of, so she calls you out, suggesting I'm being burgled. What she really hopes is that you'll find me in my pit with a lover. She thinks that would embarrass me and help her to stir up shit. It's a pity she's made a hash. It's only my brother.'

'I see, miss,' said the policeman. 'Then someone did climb through your window.'

'I've just told you,' said Julie, twisting her shoulders to give him a flash of breast, 'but only my brother.'

The other policeman cleared his throat.

'This brother of yours, can we see him now? Sounds like funny business it all does, especially if as you suggest, miss, he's your lover too. There's a law against that.'

'There's a law against most things,' said Julie.

'And so there ought to be.'

And Colin had come through, blundering drunk.

'What is all this?' he exclaimed. 'Why, Officer Krupke, you're really a square.'

'Hi kid, feeling better?' Julie said. 'These cops seem to think you're a burglar, brother.'

'No burglar I.'

'This young lady says you're her brother, is that the case . . . ?'

'Well,' said Colin sitting down abruptly on the floor, 'you know how these things are.'

And he had fallen momentarily asleep.

'You're sure you're all right miss?' said Policeman A, suddenly revealing himself as the sympathetic half of the duo. 'Sure you can manage him?'

'I'm used to my brother.'

'Brother, huh,' said the one who had been cast as the abrasive tough guy.

'But maybe you could help me get him to a couch.'

The policemen had seized Colin willingly, Abrasive twisting his arm sufficiently fiercely to cause him to open his eyes and exclaim,

'Gee Officer Krupke, give us a break . . . in the opinion of this court this guy don't need his head shrunk at all . . .'

'You've got a lovely brother, miss. He's trouble.'

And they chucked him on the couch.

'We'll keep our eye on you, miss,' said Abrasive.

'You look after yourself, miss,' said Sympathetic. 'If you've any trouble we're in the book . . .'

'That's sweet of you,' said Julie, locking the door behind them.

'Quels clowns,' said Colin.

They started laughing, giggling hopelessly and ten minutes later were making love.

'Puppyish love,' said Julie.

It wasn't a bad start to a relationship and they were married a month later. Nobody could quite say why, except that they felt like it. Worse reasons doubtless exist.

They were together for several years, always, it seemed, laughing; no couple more fun to visit. Then it was less so, and they were often separate, first because Julie was working in Rep somewhere in the North. She began to be serious about her career, was overheard once speaking of Ibsen; then came back to London with a part in an ever-running TV soap-opera (bad girl with a heart of gold). She slept with the producer, the casting-director and two or three of the other stars. 'We girls get hassled, but boy do we get on,' she said to Belinda, only part mocking herself. The truth was, Belinda thought, that Julie liked sex and Colin didn't.

His career, if you could call it that, foundered. From Cambridge he went into advertising, still just fashionable, though the Media was already the preferred goal of the real high-fliers. But Colin's choice suggested that his nostalgia had settled for the early nineteen fifties, one of his spiritual periods in a curious way Belinda had never quite managed to analyse. A false move however; there was nothing for him there. His lack of dynamism and contempt for enthusiasm soon saw him out. He embarked on a succession of temporary expedients. He sold bad German champagne on commission, tried to market a check-weighing machine a friend had invented, briefly ran an art gallery to the point of bankruptcy (its owner, a middle-aged Frenchwoman, had felt a tendresse for him); squired American tourists around stately homes; taught in two Prep Schools and three language schools; worked in the odd pub. He had no difficulty in getting jobs; keeping them was more arduous and he had never cared for the arduous.

Inherited money had kept the wolf at a distance from the door, but inflation was eating up his capital. Now it seemed Julie's career also was in decline—Belinda had last seen her the worse for gin in a Fulham Road pub, being embraced by a negress in a pink skirt. It seemed a long way from the boy and girl laughing in puppyish love.

She said, 'Colin, I want to go to bed, God knows what time it is . . .'

There was new light growing in the sky, the bottle was nearly empty and the fingers which touched her face were chill.

Colin said, 'Two thousand pounds a year, what the hell has happened to the poor girl? I mean when I was last in London I borrowed a hundred from her, so she knows my condition. Anyway God knows what she earns, has she an expensive lover?'

Belinda had the impression that Julie's tastes might have changed, that political convictions might have been instilled in her, convictions which would encourage her to demand money from Colin whether she needed it or not. But it might be that her career had really foundered. It happened to actresses, especially, she assumed, those like Julie who depended more on girlish prettiness—an early and veritable dolly-bird—than on any genuine dramatic talent. They were deciduous trees; theatrical summers could be brief and autumns keen.

'Of course,' said Colin, 'this place will make a difference.'

'You think Grace will leave it to you . . . ?'

'My dear, it's not Grace's to leave. Grandpa Major only left it to her for life, then it comes to me.'

Belinda didn't know what to make of this revelation. Colin was a liar and very drunk, capable of saying (and believing) anything; it might equally be true. After all, it raised a possibility that had never occurred to her. Had Colin been sleep-walking for years towards a certain destination?

'O.K.,' she said, 'I still want to go to bed.'

At last she lay there, listening to bird-song and unable to sleep. Remind me to tell you about his wife . . . it is fear, little brother, it is fear, but lovely are the curves of the white owl sweeping and once out of nature I shall never take my bodily form . . . the light grew in the room, light of the early dawn of the summer North, flickering through the gap in the curtain, picking up the smile on the boy's face as he leant, acanthus-crowned, against the lone Corinthian column.

II

Two weeks passed. Belinda's routine of life was dominated by her attendance in the sick-room. Grace was weaker every day, only able to converse for a few minutes at a time, less and less clear in her thought, more and more inclined to drift into the past. Most of the time Belinda just sat by the bed. She couldn't read while she sat there and had the idea, incongruous to her, that she ought to be knitting. There was a lot of time to think; not much that she wanted to think about.

Annie took over for a spell in the afternoon and in the evening while Belinda had something to eat. It wasn't necessary for anyone to be there at night, after Grace had had her last pills. She slept through the night. Grace was always restive though after Annie had been with her—Belinda had a sudden, surely lunatic, notion that Annie sat there abusing her dying sister, casting up the accumulated bitterness of a lifetime at her, all she had ever venomously wanted to say, but dared not.

Colin looked into the sick-room two or three times a day; no more; and with nothing to say. What could he be expected to find?

Their brother Andrew telephoned from his London flat, where he lived his secret, successful life, based on what he had once imparted to Belinda: 'the secret of life is simply self'.

Dr Craig called daily. Belinda found herself looking forward to taking coffee with him; every day they seemed to get nowhere. It was like finding themselves on a fair-ground animal, going round and round, with no destination, no progress even. The fishing expedition never took place. At the last moment Belinda had telephoned to say she didn't think she could manage it; no explanation. Patrick Craig had merely said, 'I'm sorry about that; perhaps some other time.' He had brought them four trout that he had caught. Belinda had asked him to stay for supper and help eat them. He had excused himself; it seemed to her unlikely that they would ever go fishing together. Nor had she reminded Fiona to tell her about his wife, even though there had been enough opportunity. She could have found opportunity for anything on Fiona's half-dozen visits, so emptily, desert-like, did their conversation stretch. But there was no coming-together; without that how could she ask for what would at best be gossip? They couldn't talk about their mother's absence either; Fiona still stood in awe of her.

Martin paid no visits. She heard that he had gone to Ireland to buy cattle, that he was involved in hectic political activity, that he was always on the point of coming. But he didn't. Annie remarked on this. 'You've quarrelled, I suppose,' she sniffed. 'He was for ever here before you came.'

'No, we haven't quarrelled.'

But in some way she had let Martin down. It was as if he had awaited her arrival in hope, expecting from her some sort of release from the tensions which gripped him. She hadn't been able to offer it. Martin had seen what he had hoped for as a mere delusion—he had therefore taken refuge in activity. But it might not be like that at all . . .

Kenneth, however, came twice. They were both shy. The first time he came it was with the protection of an errand of Fiona's. Belinda had taken him down stairs, not to the kitchen which she associated with long nocturnal conversations with Colin, but to a small sitting-room, now little used, which looked out at the side of the house to a small lawn, fringed with rose-bushes and enclosed by laurels. She had left him there while she went to make tea.

He was admiring a cage of stuffed birds when she returned with the tray.

'I loved those as a girl,' she said.

'I like them now.'

'A bit moth-eaten, wouldn't you say?'

'Part of their charm perhaps. Blessedly unplastic.'

'That was my favourite'—she pointed to a black and yellow bird—'we were told it was a Malayan Robin; it seems unlikely . . .'

56

'Humming-birds are always a bit of a disappointment.'

'Especially when stuffed . . . have some tea and cucumber sandwiches. Clever of me don't you think to find them in the market and have ready money for them . . .'

She couldn't be sure that he took the allusion. Perhaps, though, he simply found it too obvious . . .

They sat in silence for a moment, then began to talk, not, for a long time, as far as she could remember afterwards, about anything. Which was a relief, simply to chat. She had always loved chatting; so, it seemed, did Kenneth . . .

The second time he came Belinda had had a bad morning. She had come into Grace's bedroom, attracted there by the sound of a raised voice, to find Annie abusing her sister; she was indeed screaming at her.

'Always the favoured one, nothing but the best good enough and living filthily, while as for me . . .'

'What is this?' said Belinda, 'What are you trying to do? What on earth do you think you are doing, have you gone mad . . .?'

'That's what you'd like to think, isn't it?' Annie turned on her, 'I know what you've been plotting, you needn't think I don't know what you two discuss, what you get up to together . . . you're as evil as she is, but the Lord is not blind, God is not mocked . . .'

Belinda looked down at Grace; her fingers were gripping the counterpane, the veins standing out blue and the nails white. Her lips were bluish too and there was a film over her eyes. She moved just the tip of her tongue forward and touched her lips. Then they moved as she tried to form words, but no sound came.

Belinda said to Annie, 'Stop it, just stop it at once.'

Annie looked very small standing leaning over the bed. Belinda didn't dare to put her hand on her and turn her round and out of the room. She had to do it by words. For a long moment Annie made no response; only a little hissing sound. Belinda was afraid that if she touched her, if she tried

57

to turn her round and out, Annie would fight, would claw and would start screaming again.

Click, just like a slide show (holiday snaps) the picture changed. Annie sniffed, twice, pursed her mouth, made a sound as if sucking a jujube, and then, with quick precise tittuping steps, marched daintily out of the room, not closing the door, but going quick, brisk, precise, down the stairs. Her steps died away, growing fainter on the parquet floor.

Belinda looked down. Grace lay there, for a moment like an effigy on a Gothic tomb. Then, ever so slightly, the fingers relaxed their grip, the tongue moistened the lips and the eyes cleared. She couldn't smile though. Yet Belinda knew that was what she was attempting. She sat down beside her and took her hand. It was icy. She held it, rubbing gently, talking gently, saying she couldn't afterwards remember what, but whatever the words were, her intention was effective. She could sense Grace being soothed as love breathed its thawing breath on the frost of hatred. Love, she thought, is the true Sun God, Apollo made flesh.

They stayed like that into the afternoon. Belinda didn't dare move. If she took her hand away Grace would die. She was sure of it. Only her hand's cement held Grace there; that and the double string on which their eyes were threaded. All, even the bird-song outside, was held in suspense. They passed through the noon-day hour, sun at its zenith, the heavy hour of the Greeks, when the temples were deserted.

And, amazingly, looking out, as if for the first time, she saw that the sky was a deep Mediterranean blue, and felt that it was hot. That accounted, of course, for the hush. The temples untrodden; there was a word—Greek too?—for it; *controra*, the ominous hour. At this hour, it was said, as at midnight, spirits walked abroad. It came back to her, as from a distant memory and another country . . . '*Non timebis a timore nocturno; a sagitta volante in die; a negotio perambulante in tenebris; ab incursu et demonio meridiano.*' And she found herself saying these words.

And as long as she sat there, and could see neither grass

58

nor leaves, none of the northern verdance, but only this astonishing blue sky, so long she inhabited that other country.

And she could not move, could not withdraw her hand to change the mood; for very fear.

Nor could she contemplate it—let fear in and love is weakened. Weaken love and Grace will die . . .

She was interrupted. A dry, hacking, choking cough. Ridiculously she looked down at Grace, ridiculously because it was too loud and anyway came from outside the room. For a moment she thought it was Annie, and prepared to tell her to go away. But of course it wasn't; it was Colin, home from the lunch-time pub.

'Hi,' he said, 'how's tricks?'

He advanced towards the bed, raffish yet elegant, his face almost concerned. Belinda shook her head very slightly.

He lowered his voice to a whisper. 'Asleep?'

She could smell the whisky; it didn't offend her, for it banished that demon and spoke of sociability.

'Want me to take over?' he whispered.

She shook her head again.

'Young Kenneth came up with me from the village. To see you, not me. Though he didn't say . . . he's down in the hall now.'

Belinda indicated that Colin should come closer. She whispered, 'Ask him if he can wait a little. Then telephone and see if you can get Patrick Craig. Ask him to come. Then maybe come back for a moment. O.K. . ?'

Colin nodded, the whisky light in his eyes dulling. He glanced down at Grace and put his hand on Belinda's shoulder and squeezed. She couldn't remember when he had last touched her. For a long time she knew that Colin had avoided physical contact, when he could. She had watched with amusement how he evaded Fiona's determined conventional sisterly embrace.

She was glad Kenneth had come, that she hadn't done anything last time to alarm him—she was sure that wouldn't be difficult, sure partly because she thought of him as a cat.

The sunlight was hitting the bed now and she ought to get up and draw the curtain across before it touched Grace's cheek and got in her eye. She should have asked Colin to do that, it would help the banishing too; but she dared not release the fingers which, just and very occasionally, moved slightly as if they were trying to squeeze.

Suddenly she knew it was afternoon; the sun was beginning to come down the sky, the *controra* was completed. And *controra* was, of course, Italian not Greek—the counter hour —how could she have been so bemused as to think it Greek? They were into a gentler time, which was also lazy and languorous. Colin, at sixteen or seventeen, used to quote to her annoyance, for cricket bored her stiff, something of Cardus's about, she thought, Trent Bridge: 'a land where it is always afternoon and 345 for 3'. She knew why it appealed; as good as lotos, she supposed.

Grace was sleeping; naturally now. All tension that Annie had generated was relaxed. Belinda very gently withdrew her hand and got to her feet. She went to the window. Colin and Kenneth were lying on the lawn, Kenneth on his back with a stem of grass between his lips, Colin sitting with his legs drawn up and a cigarette in his hand; he had a bottle of wine and a glass in front of him. He was clearly talking; she wondered what on earth about and whether Kenneth was listening or just letting his thoughts be annihilated in the blue of the summer sky. At that moment Colin looked up, saw her standing there and made a gesture, a quick flick of his wrist to be unfailingly interpreted by all those who were, or ever had been, even honorary members of what he so easily called the great brotherhood of alcohol. She smiled and raised a hand, but did not offer to descend. She couldn't abandon her vigil, not while Annie was presumably loose in the house. Colin must have said something, for Kenneth rolled over on to his elbows, his loose unbuttoned grey shirt swinging free to hang to the grass like a bedspread, and from this position contrived to raise his head high enough to get her in sight and smile. He waved a hand and then pushed it into his hair, as if embarrassed by the temerity of this commitment, a warm greeting; he lay there poised, the upper half of his trunk supported by one point, that thin elbow.

She gestured for one of them—Kenneth she hoped—to come up. They exchanged a couple of sentences—she wants one of us, can't be bothered, you go, no you go, happy in this sun, sunning myself, you go, it's you she wants—and in the end Kenneth got, more lethargically than she might have wished, to his feet, and moved in his tight blue jeans and loose shirt like a splay-legged stork across the daisied lawn and into the shadow of the house. He was, she noticed now, dangling a daisy-chain from his left wrist. She liked him for that.

She went to the door and listened to the house breathing until she heard his light step on the stair.

Belinda holds her hand up in the dark cool hallway at the top of the stairs, the landing. She looks at it a moment in wonder as a hand that in the last hours has worked more effectively than in all its hours that have gone before. She extends it towards Kenneth coming up the stairs, his steps moving in concert with her heartbeats. She feels tears prick her eyes; she would like to be herself taken in arms and embraced, hard, with life. That is not what Kenneth will do. She has no right to ask him or to intimate that this is what she desires. She draws back; picture of a lady at the stairhead. Kenneth stops short of the top step. He speaks in a low voice.

'Colin said to say the doctor'll be here as soon as he can. Whenever that is, Colin says.'

'I can't leave her,' she says. 'She's had a bad turn. It was nice of you to come. I'm sorry . . .'

More sorry than I can say, I who have always professed indifference for decorum.

'Can you stay a bit longer? Maybe after the doctor has been, we can have some tea, take a walk or something, I've got a headache from sitting in the sick-room.'

This is a lie and she can't account for it. Headache is not what she has.

'Of course, I've nothing to do, what would I have to . . . only I think Fiona may be coming over. If she does I'll probably evaporate.'

'Oh sure. I understand.'

And it is horrible how much she understands.

At that moment the telephone rings; she is sure it will be Patrick Craig . . .

'Can you stay here? Don't let anyone in. Not anyone.'

If Kenneth thinks this instruction odd, he gives no sign of it. Perhaps he doesn't. Kenneth has enough distrust of others to accept it as normal.

It is jarring, the noise of the telephone in the dead afternoon of the hall. She runs downstairs lest it wake Grace.

Only it is not Patrick, but her brother Andrew . . .

'And how are things?' says Andrew. 'No deaths in the family yet darling?'

'Don't joke about it . . .'

'Sound rather tense . . .'

'And why not . . . what the hell are you doing about it?'

'Nothing, as is my wont, I have other fish to fry, not that you'll want to hear about that. Oh no. No, the thing is, do you want me to come up yet because if you do, I'll do it, well, I'll even put up with Colin . . .'

Andrew has always been jealous of Colin; it persists even now, even though Andrew is in his creepy way a success, while Colin . . .

'No,' says Belinda, 'there's no need.'

'In your element are you?' says Andrew. 'No don't take off, Bel, that's not my view of things, it's our bitch of a mother. That's what she said to me yesterday—"Of course," she said, "Belinda and Colin are having a lovely time keeping it all to themselves. They were always Grace's favourites," the old bag said—she's right there of course, darling, the old whited sepulchre never had any time for little me and who could for fab fashy Fiona?—"and of course they'll be having a lovely time being children again in their never-never land of country pleasures." Quite an articulate outburst from the fashion editor, wouldn't you say? What a bitch she is, but on the ball. Talking of which, balls I mean, little Mike's had his clipped—I mean she's through with him, a searing scaring row in St Trops apparently and he walked off with a piece of Froggie tail. What a fury, but only on the surface. Of course she provoked the row, the poor brute was quite shagged out. So . . .'

'Look Andrew, I've got to go. Grace has had a bad turn today, that lunatic Annie . . .'

'Aunt Annie is no lunatic, she knows what she wants to get . . .'

'So did Hitler . . .'

'Never heard that anyone certified him, ducky.'

'So I must fly, besides I left only Kenneth watching over Grace . . . you remember Kenneth, our ghastly brother-in-law Gavin's little brother . . .'

'Of course I remember Kenneth, is he about, give him my love won't you, what I wanted to warn you though before you hang up, two things. One, the old bitch's new boy is even worse—Kevin and comes from Stockport, quel dredging of gutters—two, I met your appalling ex-husband yesterday in Harrods—you'd think they'd have some sort of discrimination in Harrods but they let simply anybody in—I thought I'd warn you he's coming to Scotland and verb sap he was speaking so *simpaticamente* and understandingly about you. Does that warm the cockles of your heart? Does it make you cry cockles and muscles alive alive oh, and so au voir darling, don't forget to give my love to Kenneth and of course Grace. That one's a piece of prospective gaiety if ever I saw one, not Grace silly, Bye, bye, bye . . .'

No, no, no, that was what in the end you had to reply to Andrew, about almost everything.

And yet she conveys his love to Kenneth, whom she finds leaning like a chorus-boy on the bedroom doorpost; his face clouds over, but it may be a trick of the light, ever so uncertain in the hall and on the landing.

'There's been no sound from Grace,' he says, and she is

63

again pleased he finds it natural to call her Grace. 'I looked in quickly just once and she's sleeping.'

'Thank you very much,' she says, and looks at him, trying to be certain of displeasure not embarrassment in his face a moment since; but that expression has of course vanished as he speaks of Grace; silly of her to look for it again, to search for something as fleeting as revelation . . .

Evening. Colin is sitting with Grace. He has a bottle of claret with him, but is sober enough, and Grace is in a drugged sleep. All he must do is ward Annie off. Even though she enters there is nothing she can say that Grace will now hear. Nothing either has been seen of Annie for hours; she has retired to her room.

Belinda and Patrick Craig are in the kitchen.

She is about to make an omelette.

'I wish you'd let me take you out,' he says, 'steak would be better for you than eggs.'

'Make me sick. Besides I couldn't face going out.'

'I'll fix up a nurse,' he says for the third time. 'It's got to the stage when it's too much for you, since there's no one to share it with you.'

She doesn't protest, doesn't offer Colin, though she is not made nervous by the thought that he is in charge now.

'I suppose money's all right,' she says, '. . . aren't nurses expensive? . . . oh yes, money will be all right. Silly of me to think otherwise. Silly. I'm sorry.'

She slides the first omelette onto a plate and takes it to him.

'Eat it at once,' she says, 'before it becomes like rubber.'

There is a bubbling sound from the coffee and she moves the pot off the Aga's ring, and then pours the other eggs into the pan. When they are ready she pours coffee into two little mugs (gaily-patterned Deruta mugs she once brought Grace from Perugia) and puts one in front of Patrick.

'Sugar on the table,' she says, and sits down beside him, with the angle of the table between them, and her coffee and omelette in front of her. She sits a moment with her fork poised. Patrick is eating with enthusiasm.

'It's very good,' he says, 'you make an excellent omelette, you ought to eat yours.'

'Oh yes,' she says.

It is cool and half-dark in the kitchen which has an arched roof and stone-flagged floor. A black cat snoozes at the back of the Aga, an orange one on the window-ledge.

There might be nobody else in the house. Belinda feels unutterably heavy. She pushes her half-eaten omelette away and sips coffee and lights a Gauloise.

'About Annie,' she says at last.

Patrick says, 'I'll tell her she's got to keep clear.'

'Can you do that?'

'She won't like it. But I think she'll get the message. She wouldn't like her behaviour to become public.'

'She's got a vicious tongue herself, you know. Scandal's her meat and drink . . . Scandal and mischief-making. Do you think she's mad?'

Patrick Craig shrugs as if indifferent, but at that moment his face slides into evening shadows.

'What's mad?' he says.

'What you can find two doctors to certify, I've always understood,' says Belinda.

Two days later, leaving the nurse that Patrick had swiftly organized, in charge, Belinda walked through the woods and fields towards Fiona's. It would be her first visit since the dinner. She didn't deceive herself; it was Kenneth she hoped to see. The visit was prompted by a telephone call from Oswald. He would be there the next morning. She felt she could more easily face him if she saw Kenneth today. She had been tempted to ask them all over, to use Fiona and Gavin as shields. In the end though the idea was distasteful. At least she had had the strength to tell Oswald he wouldn't be able to stay.

Fiona was sitting on a teak bench on the lawn, watching

her children play. It made, Belinda couldn't help thinking, a charming picture; not quite Raeburn but certainly Millais.

'Well, this is a surprise,' said Fiona.

'It's such a lovely day.' Belinda glanced up at the blue sky, laced with tiny wisps of cloud.

Fiona's face had taken on a frown, it seemed to Belinda. Well, she hadn't ever been promised fatted calves.

'What have you been doing to poor old Annie?' said Fiona. You could see her chin jut out as she determinedly grasped the nettle. 'It's really very selfish of you. The poor old thing's terribly upset.'

Belinda sat down on the grass, near Fiona's feet, which others might have eschewed as a tactical error, and said nothing. Instead she plucked a stem of grass and nibbled it.

'After all,' said Fiona, 'she's been looking after Granny by herself for long enough. And it hasn't been easy. I don't suppose you'll believe that—you've always thought the sun rose and set on Granny—but she's not been easy. In fact, she's often extremely difficult, and when you think what Aunt Annie's given up, her own house, all her friends, everything really, well all I can say is I think you've been very thoughtless and selfish. She's really terribly cut up.'

This is indeed all Fiona can say, but she finds different ways of saying it, and proceeds to run through her repertory for some minutes. All the time Belinda says nothing, not bothered to defend herself—and how anyway can you defend yourself when you have only the truth that will not be believed? So she sits, head more or less bowed, twisting her fingers in the grass, throwing back the children's red-and-yellow striped ball when they kick it over, and at last lighting a cigarette.

'Well,' says Fiona, eventually, 'I've had my say and no doubt it's water off a duck's back, but you really ought to consider how poor Annie feels. Would you like some tea?'

'Yes,' says Belinda, 'I'd love that,' and Fiona goes off to make it, leaving Belinda thinking how wrong she has been not to tell Fiona what had happened, even though she wouldn't have believed it; she should have been given the chance. But she knows also she won't, when she returns. Instead she drinks up this extraordinary sun, this flowering of summer, and watches her niece and nephew, affectionately but without interest.

Fiona comes back with a tea-tray, walking elegantly even in sandals. The tea is not so good, not the Lapsang Belinda likes to drink, but some nondescript brew, probably bagged —tea, like wine, is low on Fiona's scale, far less important than hair and raiment.

'Have you heard from Mummy?' Fiona says. There is a hint of nervousness in her voice.

Belinda shakes her head. 'Not directly,' she says, 'we're not of course great communicators.'

'I'm surprised she hasn't come up. Of course she's busy.'

'Andrew telephoned a couple of days ago. He said she has no immediate plans.'

'Oh Andrew.'

'Yes.'

Fiona gives a little cough. Belinda feels herself stiffen. Really, it is ridiculous to feel nervous, because one's little sister, whom one doesn't particularly like or respect (certainly not in the way one respects those one truly respects) should, by coughing, be girding up her loins to make some pronouncement, probably impertinent, or broach, without delicacy, some delicate subject. So Belinda feels a fool and inadequate. All the same, she feels apprehensive too, and wishes Fiona had really cause to clear her throat.

Which she now does again.

'Tell me, Belinda, when it's over, when Granny's, well, dead,'—the word hangs there a moment, isolated, like a bloodstain on a white sheet—'what are your plans?'

'Plans,' says Belinda, as if the word is some strange neologism that must be inspected and weighed up before it can be admitted to the vocabulary. 'Plans,' she repeats, turning it over.

'Yes, plans. As far as I can see,' (this is a favourite expression of Fiona's, she recalls, one of those expressions where the words have quite abandoned their original meaning, for there is no suggestion that Fiona accepts any limit to her vision). 'As far as I can see,' says Fiona, 'since your marriage broke up, which is of course entirely your affair, but which made Gavin and I very sorry, because . . .'

'Gavin and me,' says Belinda.

'What?'

'Gavin and me, not Gavin and I; made Gavin and me; it's in the accusative. You wouldn't say, made I, would you?'

Fiona blushes. It is very becoming. When she is embarrassed she looks younger, and Belinda is reminded how pretty Fiona had been at sixteen.

'I'm sorry,' she says, 'priggish of me, nobody cares about grammar now,' which makes it worse somehow, and for a moment she would like to touch Fiona.

'But I do,' says Fiona, 'I think it terribly important. I can't stand this casualness about split infinitives.'

Perhaps they can talk about linguistic solecisms till Kenneth perhaps appears.

But alas no.

'Anyway,' Fiona says, 'as I was saying, we were very sorry, Gavin and . . .' she pauses '. . . I, because we thought a lot of Oswald, for all his obvious rough corners.'

This is ridiculous; there are no rough corners on smooth polished plastic.

'But,' Fiona continues, 'you can't just mope. I expect there were rights and wrongs on both sides, but you're my sister, so of course we're both on yours.'

'It wasn't like that at all,' says Belinda, hoping to stem the flow, but it turns out, this flow is not really what concerns Fiona.

'The thing is, since it happened, you don't seem to have done anything. Heaven knows what you're living on, though I suppose Oswald has to give you something, which is only right, even if, in similar circumstances, which couldn't of course happen, I wouldn't want to take it. I mean, it's not as if he's responsible, and, for a girl of your talents—oh

68

neither Gavin nor ... I ... doubts that you have talent—there are plenty of jobs, but as far as I can gather, you just sit in London, in Fulham too which I've never thought much of a place, and just do ... nothing. I suppose you mope. And it isn't good for you. I've seen the type that turns into. What worries me, Belinda, is if you go on like this, you'll end up like Colin.'

There it is, Fiona has got it out and is able to drink tea. Mysteriously no black cloud has eclipsed the sun, as this frightful fate is forecast. The sad thing is, Fiona is quite right. There have been mornings in Fulham when Belinda has only been able to force herself out of bed by the same threat. And there have been too many grey afternoons, empty when the lunchtime pubs closed, when she has turned wearily to a largely deserted cinema, merely to get through the barren hours. She would be touched by Fiona's concern, that Fiona has sensed her predicament, if she weren't simultaneously irritated by what is also presumption and impertinence.

On the other hand, there is nothing she can say in exculpation, and it's not a topic from which she can somehow depart at a tangent.

So she says nothing.

Fiona puts down her tea-cup, which is the better, but not the best, Worcester.

'Are you fixed to go back to London?' she says, 'I mean is it really necessary?'

'Necessary?' says Belinda vaguely, 'oh necessity calls me nowhere.'

'Quite. The thing is, I've had an idea. It's only a suggestion.'

The interruption Belinda has been hoping for, which is by this time any interruption, now comes. A car is heard coming up the drive.

'But what a coincidence,' Fiona says, 'now that's what I really call a coincidence.'

The car, a Mercedes, draws up and Colonel Morgan gets out of the passenger's seat. His chauffeur, a Negro, remains in his place, only settles his peaked cap to shield his eyes.

Colonel Morgan advances across the lawn with light, stalking step. He is wearing khaki drill trousers and an olive-green safari jacket, that, unlike most safari jackets, looks as if it might have experience of the bush. This appearance is supported by the cartridges that protrude from the top breast pocket. His hair is rather longer than you would expect, not greying at all, and Belinda wonders what he uses; it is obviously touched up. His eyes, which she recalls as hooded hawk's eyes, are hidden by dark dark glasses. He comes up to them and sits on the bench beside Fiona, keeping those glasses directed towards Belinda. She can see thick tufts of hair at the V of his open shirt; this hair is slightly grizzled. There is more hair, thick and black, on the hand which he rests on the arm of the bench. A heavy gold signet ring glints in the sunlight.

'I was just saying,' Fiona says, 'what a coincidence.'

'Coincidence,' says Morgan sceptically. 'Betty,' he says, 'is no good. I can't stand neurotic bitches. Throw a bucket of water over them, but you can't do that in this part of the globe, eh?'

'I told you, Betty had her faults, Gerald.'

'Gin bein' one of 'em, eh?'

'Now that I didn't know, though I won't say I haven't had my suspicions.'

All the time Morgan is not looking at Fiona but keeping those glasses fixed on Belinda, who can't meet the glasses, her gaze getting no higher than Morgan's mouth. It's not a very nice mouth.

'Would you like some tea, Gerald?'

'Never touch the stuff. Had too much when I was a boy in the desert. Lived on brew-ups, or so memory tells me, ha. Prefer a whisky-and-soda, if I may.'

'Of course, I'll . . .'

'No, you won't, don't trouble your pretty self, Kwame can fetch it, if you've no objection. Assure you, you can trust him with the liquor, much as his life's worth to forfeit that trust, much though he'll be tempted, ha. O.K.?'

He raises his hands over his right shoulder and claps twice.

Belinda is amazed to see the door of the Mercedes open and the tall white-coated Negro get out and come deferentially across the lawn.

'Whisky-soda, boy,' says Morgan, not looking at him.

'Yes, Colonel sir. Right away.'

'I'd a call from Mansie Niven,' says Fiona. 'He very much wants to meet you, Gerald.'

'Niven, eh. You know I've no time for these straw men, elected puppets.'

Morgan throws his head back as he says this. A gesture of defiance, unhappily-theatrical.

'The parliamentary game's finished,' he says, 'if the jackass can't see that, I've no time for him. What do you think of it all, lady?' He swoops towards Belinda, though in fact he does no more than jerk his head.

'I, I've no opinion on these matters.'

The answer doesn't displease him. He gives a half-smile.

'Had too much of what you think these matters are with your precious ex-husband, eh?'

This surprises Belinda, though she is at the same time relieved not to feel any residual loyalty to Oswald, not to defend him against the imputation of the word 'precious', which is not anyway used as she might use it.

'Oh you know Oswald?' is all she says.

'Oswald and I have corresponded for some time,' he surprises her again by saying, 'and though I say, "precious" it may surprise you to learn that I've a lot of time for Oswald. We started from very different points, but we're coming to the same sort of answers. We both know things can't go on as they are and we both believe in hierarchy. That's a lot of common ground, wouldn't you say?'

Belinda has a moment of understanding.

'Oh,' she says, 'I suppose you're the business that Oswald's coming up here for.'

'In one,' says Morgan, and, sensing rather than seeing the return of Kwame, he stretches out his hand to receive the glass of whisky-and-soda, which Kwame puts there. Then the servant backs two or three steps and turns and walks

71

back to the car. His shoulders are seen to be stooped. No words are exchanged. Belinda watches Kwame back to the Mercedes, while Morgan takes two or three sips of his drink. In the car, Kwame again tilts the peaked cap, which he had discarded to go on his drinks mission, over his eyes, and seems to resume sleep.

'You see,' says Morgan, 'we're both past talk, and,' he chuckles, 'since we neither of us see violence as a suitable means of pressing to the next stage of social organization—at this stage, that's to say, though'—does he really lick his curiously thin lips?—'the time for that may come, we have to create some sort of organization we can use. It's really a matter of being in the education business, you know, Fiona. Social education.'

Belinda looks round the desperate garden to where the roses run into the rhododendrons. Only God can make a tree, but men play hell with abc—someone has stabbed a knife into the feather mattress of vocabulary and Belinda is being smothered by the feathered words let loose.

'The immediate question is,' says Morgan, 'whether we can use you. You're at a loose end, I gather, or will be again soon. Oswald thinks we can. Fiona here thinks we can. I'm, I confess, doubtful. I'd need to be convinced.'

'I'm not sure of what I have to convince you, but I can't really see why I should want to,' says Belinda. She looks him straight in the dark glasses. 'I didn't hear what you had to say the other night,' she says. 'I didn't choose to.'

'You're spoiled, of course,' he says. 'You're a lovely woman and you're spoiled.'

Gerald Morgan is clearly the sort of man who has given himself the right to say anything. Belinda glances at Fiona to see how she receives this. Fiona's lips are slightly parted, her eyes shine like a girl at her second corrida when the torero she has returned to see executes a perfect veronica.

'How would you know?' says Belinda, her fingers pushing vaguely at her thighs.

Morgan chuckles. 'But spunky,' he says. 'I need an administrative assistant,' he says. 'Interested? How about it?' He lowers his voice and it becomes a little American, 'Give it a go, eh?'

'Do you think he's mad, or just nasty?' she asked Colin later.

'Wanted for rape in seven countries and genocide in Outer Mongolia, where men are men and they don't normally trouble about such things.'

'*E vero?*'

'Cross my heart and hope to die.'

At the time, feeling Morgan's eyes strip her from their lair behind the glasses, she had got to her feet, and standing for a moment in the gauche attitude of a clothed Botticelli Venus, said something or other, in self-excuse, to Fiona. The nurse would soon be off duty, something like that.

'Kwame'll run you back, eh?'

'No, he won't,' she said. 'Thank you all the same.'

She turned and made off to walk, going as if by the village.

What would she have done if he had offered to accompany her?

But he didn't. Not his style.

But if he had?

The thought stayed with her into the wood. She felt a little sick. A phrase, floating to her from a gang of street corner louts in Fulham a few weeks back, came to her; 'you can tell she does by the way she walks'. She looked back over her shoulder. A strand of hair blew into her mouth and over her eyes. She pushed it away, and then pushed again, with fingers that were urgent and sweaty, at her jeaned thighs. She almost ran, turned round again, but behind, the wood closed in silent and undemanding. A stray briar caught and tore her cheek, and putting her finger to it and then to her mouth, she tasted blood.

She emerged, stumbling, into the lane as a Range Rover came round the corner. It drew up beside her. She stopped,

73

blood still on her cheek, hair blown over her open mouth, and breasts rising and falling, and looked up to see Martin leaning out of the window.

'Came over a bit fast, didn't you, Bel? I say, you all right?'

She nodded.

'Want a lift? Jump in.'

She went round the front of the car, brushed through the long grasses on the bank and obeyed.

'I tripped in the fence,' she said.

'What about your face?'

'Oh my face, some bloody briar, nothing dramatic.'

'I see,' he said, 'all the same.'

'Nothing I tell you.'

She looked up, gave him a quick smile, and 'Don't be silly, Martin.'

'What have you been doing?' she said. 'We haven't seen you in a bit.'

He started up the engine.

'Well, no,' he said, 'a matter of diplomacy, you might say.'

Belinda at once knew quite well what he meant. Yet if he could only approach it obliquely she didn't see how she could bring matters into the open. The absurdity of jealousy was so often part of the fact.

'Tell me,' she said, looking down at Martin's confident cavalry-twilled leg, 'this Colonel Morgan that Fiona's so taken with, what do you make of him . . . ?'

'Something pretty unsavoury.' Martin spoke with decision and no hesitation; there was clearly no need to carry the diffidence and embarrassment of personal relations into this sort of business. 'I've good reason to believe he's an ex-mercenary, way back from the Congo days.'

'Not so pukka as he'd like to make out?'

'No, not that—pukka all right, I should say—I mean family, school, even, I believe, University, though whether before or after Sandhurst I don't know. Just caught the thirties, I'd say. No, the pukkaness is O.K.'

'So it's what?'

'If you really understand men, you don't despise them.

74

Morgan's a half-clever cynic, I don't like the type. The word
pity, which you might say is the most appropriate for the
human condition, isn't in his vocabulary.'

'Martin,' said Belinda, 'you really believe in bushels,
don't you?' Martin abruptly pulled the car off the lane and
they bumped down a rough track to the loch. He stopped on
a little knowe, an eminence which ridiculously put them
on a level with the sun, directly ahead. The radiance had
however gone out of it. It coloured the sky, red, pink, mauve,
green and yellow, but no longer dazzled. Martin lit a
cigarette.

'You prefer your own, I take it,' he said.

'Yes.'

'What do you mean, bushels?'

'Hiding your light. You know, under a bushel. You sounded
different just now. Realer in an odd way.'

'There comes a point,' Martin said, 'when it's bad manners
and bad policy to obtrude reality. Most people don't care
for it.'

'Thanks then for giving me a glimpse.'

They sat and smoked in silence, looking straight at the
sunset. Half the loch was black and a swan sailed out of that
half, the black, into the light, its feathers touched with a
lucent pink.

'Morgan was at Fiona's just now. He offered me a job and
it felt like he was threatening rape. It was nasty, nothing jolly
about it at all.'

'I can see he could have that effect.'

'He obviously fascinates Fiona, but I don't think he's
interested in her. Of course I've often thought that Fiona
. . . no, that's mean, but it's rather odd actually, when you
come to think of it, that he shouldn't be interested in her.'

('I suppose his rapery isn't crude?' said Colin later when
she put the same idea forward to him.)

'What sort of job?' said Martin.

'Oh I don't know, I didn't really listen. He talked about an
administrative assistant for some sort of social organization;
all the sort of thing that really means simply nothing, nothing,

nothing at all. The odd thing is he's in some way involved with Oswald. That means of course that even if it was the most super job, which quite clearly it isn't, I wouldn't touch it with . . . whatever it is one doesn't touch things with, barge-poles?'

'Oswald eh, you're really glad to be out of that, Bel . . . ?'

'Really glad.'

Belinda stopped; it was surely impossible to have mistaken the note of envy in Martin's voice? It was surely a note of envy?

'Well,' said Martin, 'it's one thing about being a woman, you can always just up sticks and off. Everything you need packed in a couple of suitcases.'

'Surely men can travel light?'

'Some can, but tell me this, how does a farmer leave his wife?'

Belinda paused. She ought to go on. She lit another cigarette from the first which she stubbed out in the ashtray.

'I take it that question's not entirely rhetorical?' she said at last.

'No, but I'll save you the trouble of answering it. There's no way he can, with land prices as they are, not unless he's got a lot of courage. I'll tell you how one farmer I knew left his wife—by means of a shotgun.'

'Martin . . .'

'Oh no, I'm not that sort. That's not my style, as Colin would say. Did Colin leave Julie or t'other way round?'

'I don't know, I think you could say that cookie crumbled; sheer disintegration. Does Jill know you feel like this?'

'How do I know?'

The telephone was ringing as Belinda came into the hall, and, for a moment, she was tempted to turn round and go out again, walk away till it stopped; for it was clear no one else was going to answer it. She had none of the inhibitions many felt about doing this; it was a frequent pleasure to let telephones die away. But she picked it up and immediately,

76

hearing her mother's voice, wished she had obeyed her wiser impulse.

'I'm glad it's you,' said her mother, 'it was you I wanted to speak to, what the hell do you think you're playing at?'

'You'll have to explain,' said Belinda, 'you sound as if we were in the middle of a conversation, when we're actually only starting.'

'I've had a letter from Annie.'

'Oh Annie,' she felt a weariness descend, 'well, I don't of course know what she said, but I should think it's probable you should just tear it up.'

'God, how typical, how callous and irresponsible you and Colin are.'

Belinda glanced at her wrist watch. Half-past eight, yes, she could well be, certainly was, well into the gin.

'What's Annie been saying? I'd better know,' she said.

'You don't seem to realize it but Annie has devoted years of her life to caring for Grace. Naturally she's hurt, bitterly hurt, when you come swanning up from London, and take over, exclude her from the sick-room and then spread stories which, she says, suggest that she is unbalanced. She actually said unbalanced. What's more, there's something pretty improper, bloody underhand, doing all this in collusion with a doctor who by all accounts is a good deal less than he should be. As I've said before, the trouble with you and Colin is you're too fucking pleased with yourselves for having contrived to spend all your life achieving fuck all.'

She slammed down the receiver, but Belinda stood for a moment in the hall, still holding it to her ear, as if she could hear, as in a conch, the echoing surge. She felt her mother's contempt; was amazed at her own ability to dismiss it, even perhaps rise above it. Yet, by the world's standards, as they were now, there could be no doubt about it, she and Colin— and the association was closer and more frequent than she liked—were flops; her mother, Andrew, and even Fiona, were successes. She couldn't hide that fact from herself. Colin entered the hall, light-footed, his hair flopping over his left eyebrow.

'Would you say,' Belinda said, 'we were too fucking pleased, you and I, with ourselves for having contrived to spend all our lives achieving fuck all?'

'What an extraordinary judgement. Our mother's, I take it? That was she on the telephone, was it? As I've been heard to remark, the woman's a fool. She's not coming up is she?'

'No; the only purpose of the call was to abuse me.'

'Oh well.'

'Apparently Annie has been poison-penning.'

'To be expected.'

Belinda went upstairs to relieve the nurse.

'She's been very quiet. She's hardly stirred.'

'She doesn't seem to much. She's very good.'

The truth was, Grace had no will left; she was going gentle, with no rage. Over the last days Belinda had found her own attitude moving into one of complete acceptance. It was surprising because she had long told herself there was no hope, only to have become aware, by this recent death of hope, that somehow hope had survived. Now she looked down at Grace's withered features, the hollow cheeks, yellowed with no remaining flush, the thin lips and the blank eyes and the mad straggling wisps of hair, and the thought came to her—it's time it was all over. She said to the nurse instead, 'You go and have your supper, you'll find it laid out on the kitchen table.'

'Oh it's the life of Riley, I'm leading here. I'll come back and give the old lady her night injection and bed her down.'

'That's very good of you, I'll sit with her now.'

But she had lost the intimacy of the earlier days. It was not just that Grace was weaker and drifting away, becoming so much less herself—though it was that, and the realization raised the question, when does death begin?—it was also however that the nurse's takeover, her interposition, had impaired their intimacy. Grace now was less Grace dying; she had become 'the patient', 'the old lady'.

Belinda found herself restless. She walked round the room picking up objects, holding them up, turning them in her

78

hands, and setting them down again. If Grace still had, at this moment, consciousness, it must irritate her, this fiddling and fidgeting, but Belinda couldn't help it, any more than a small child told to stop fiddling or stop fidgeting, could actually obey the instruction; instead, in fact, more often intensified the annoyance.

A photograph of the four of them as children. How insignificant Andrew was. She guessed he had a stained collar, dirty fingernails and scuffed shoes. There was something rat-like about him. He was a sleek rat these days. In contrast Colin looked debonair, on top of the world. Could a psychologist or physiognomist detect the future from this photograph? She doubted it. As for herself, she couldn't feel any connection with the demure, pig tailed little girl; yet her childhood memories were compellingly real. It made little sense. Only Fiona, sweetly pretty here, but pretty with a characterful prettiness, seemed to have her course marked out. You would predict that this little girl would be just where she was today. Did that mean that the surprise for Fiona was still to come?

For a moment, the image of Gerald Morgan, striding across the lawn in safari-jacket and high boots (which he had not in fact been wearing) flashed into her mind. But Gerald Morgan wasn't interested in Fiona.

She sat down beside Grace, but on the bed, the wrong side of the bed, where the photographs were, and picked up the one of Uncle Alastair.

'Poor dear Alastair,' Grace had said before she became too weak for conversation, 'how you would have doted on him, dear.'

How easily she could have, looking at that curving mouth and the candid gaze. Colin's blue eyes, she supposed. Yet, flawless though he looked, the mark must be there. The art to read the mind's construction in the face. A desert D.S.O., that was something to remember; when had she learned that the Normandy death-wound was in the back? Did she even know this for sure, or was it poison Andrew, for example, had distilled?

'There was a part of me never got over it,' Grace had said. 'Curiously your grandfather minded it less. He thought the world of Alastair when he was at school. After that, they drifted apart. Politics on the surface, but it went further. Of course, your grandfather was an old fool, given to striking moral attitudes. Nobody really quarrels over politics.'

'Just a neutral means of expressing distaste.'

'Yes.'

'But I would have doted and indeed I always have. It's a weakness, doting, not how one should feel about anybody.' But she hadn't said this, only thought it now, as she looked over the dark, twilit room to the dark obscurity of the vegetation without. There was no moon tonight, and it was as if, after the full-throated summer day, heavy clouds were mustering.

She wondered where Kenneth had been in the afternoon. How did he spend his time? He talked as if it hung heavy. Had he been lying somewhere drinking up the sun, fuelling his thin body with energy to see it through the winter? We were like plants, needing photo-synthesis to flourish, if photo-synthesis meant approximately what she thought it did.

How could he tolerate life there, with Fiona's debby immaturity and easy judgement, Gavin's deadly obviousness; both of them prompt to dismiss anything that contradicted their prejudices simply as 'childish' or, worst of all, 'impractical and unrealistic'. Yet all the same, Fiona and, she supposed, Gavin also, had been fascinated—stoats and rabbits—by Gerald Morgan.

But she wished Kenneth had put in an appearance, and she looked at the photograph she still held in her hand, and, in the dim light, saw the features rearrange themselves.

You can still hear the rain beat on the corrugated iron roof of the potting-shed just to the left of the kitchen window, but the thunder has passed. Grandpa Major had that roof put on to replace a broken tiled one in the year he and Grace returned to the house after the war. Ever since Grace has grumbled about it, vowed to restore the tiles, but she has never done so. After all, her inactivity has seemed to say to Belinda, what would be the point, it's not as if life is going to go on here. Quite why it shouldn't Belinda couldn't say. In fact, it certainly will. Someday, probably fairly soon, Colin will sell the place (she has now accepted that it will be his to sell); she can't see why he should wish to go on living here. It is probably too large for an academic, even a professor from the new University, but it will be bought by an executive in one of the new, oil-related industries. His suburban English or suburban, country-club, American wife, will, depending on taste and temperament, either tear the place apart, refurbish from top to bottom, in an attempt to create a mini-Surrey villa or a Connecticut week-end cottage, or she will lovingly preserve and restore. Either way though, the house as Belinda has known it, smelling of roses, pot-pourri, Turkish cigarettes, Burmese cheroots and dog, will become no more than a memory. So perhaps Grace's inactivity is justified after all.

The drumming of the rain intensifies the silence in the kitchen. Belinda begins to wonder if Colin has passed out; with his eyes open.

But no, he bestirs himself, pours more wine.

'So, your ex-husband will be with us tomorrow?' he says, voice slurred.

'That's what it looks like.'

'*Quel espèce de boue.*'

'Oh come.'

'You defend him?'

'Curiously Oswald is, in his way, all right. It just didn't happen to be my way.'

'Whose way could it be?'

'Oh I can think of several, types rather than particular people, I must admit, who might think it was.'

'Incredible. Mind you, I fail to see why I should say that. No course of action so absurd that you won't find idiots queuing up to take it. That's been my experience. Why, however, is he coming, here? Not surely to lure you back?'

'No I don't think that's the case at all. Curiously Oswald's vanity wasn't even dented when I took off. He barely noticed. No, he has other fish to fry.'

And she tells him about her meeting with Morgan only that afternoon.

'Do you think he's mad, or just plain nasty?' she asks.

'Wanted for rape in seven counties and genocide in Outer Mongolia, where men are men and they don't normally trouble about such things.'

'*E vero?*'

'Cross my heart and hope to die.'

As he says this Colin suddenly looks much younger. She can see a boy laughing.

'I shouldn't think,' he says, 'Oswald is up to his weight.'

'You underestimate Oswald, you always have. Goodness knows I know what Oswald's worth and it's not much, but he has a certain . . .'

'*Je ne sais quoi*—I shouldn't say so; me, I know exactly *quoi* the sod is worth. *E niente.*'

Belinda sighs. If only Colin could apply his talents to something other than analysis, criticism and denigration; she has thought this thought far too often before for it to be even a thought now. She has really no idea whether it corresponds either to anything outside her mind, objective reality of any kind. Still, there is something of comfort in it, as in everything that is familiar.

'How much longer do you give her?' Colin says.

Belinda is startled. 'Do you mean Grace?'

'She is, as far as I'm aware, the only one dying round here.'

'A week, maybe ten days, but Patrick says it could happen any minute. It's not something you can predict like an eclipse.'

'You'll have got rid of Oswald before it happens, I take it? I don't want him round here when it does. It would be indecorous.'

There is something extraordinary in this; it sounds as if Colin has been brooding, in genuine head of the household way, on funeral arrangements.

'I think Oswald would be a cremation man,' she says.

Colin pours more wine. 'Cremation,' he says, 'a very Bovis way to go.'

'But,' says Belinda, 'I can't control what Oswald does, his movements aren't in my charge, I'm not married to him any more and he's not coming to see me, he's coming to see this creepy Gerald Morgan. Maybe you should talk to Fiona about it, she and Gavin have a very high opinion of Oswald.'

She is surprised to find herself so angry, and the anger is certainly directed at Colin. She could happily hit him.

'Quite,' he said, 'but if he's about, he'll get short shrift from me. It was bad enough enduring him as a brother-in-law. The relationship happily being at an end, I see no reason why I should be afflicted with him further.'

She can see Colin with his back against a chimney piece, spreading his coat-tails to warm his bum at the roaring log fire, standing with his feet planted wide apart on the hearth-rug, laird, squire and paterfamilias, laying down the law, possibly proceeding to family prayers; and she begins to laugh.

'Just a bit jolly thick it would be,' he says.

'What about Andrew,' she says, 'will you let him come?'

'Andrew I can't stop. But I shall find an Andrew-tease. Andrew is vile. Andrew buggers niggers, I don't care for that.'

'I don't think he does. What he describes as business-boys is what Andrew goes in for.'

There is a note of distaste in Belinda's voice; no more. She accepts this as one of those things, though she goes on to say, if pressed, that, yes, she finds it 'a bit sordid'. Colin these days waxes strong against what he still, anachronistically perhaps, calls buggery and nancery, even though, Belinda has been told (and not only by Andrew) he used to practise it enthusiastically enough himself. There was almost a scandal in his last year at school; and the first boy Belinda made love to confessed in happy liquor, 'Year before last I was crazy about your brother.'

'Did you ever go to bed with Colin?' she had said.

'Oh yes, once, when he was staying with us in Edinburgh

83

for a dance. Too much claret-cup which we were unused to, and it . . . wasn't a success. Neither of us knew what to do. So we just romped about for a bit, and then both went to sleep. I was awfully embarrassed to find Colin there in the morning, and he was horridly cold to me all the next term. Then we both found other boy friends and made it up, and now I've found you and am finished with boys.'

It might, she now reflects, recalling the memory, be as well if what he said then is true, for he is now an Edinburgh advocate and Tory candidate. She saw him on television only yesterday. It was impossible to believe she had made love to him again as little as twelve or thirteen years before, and no doubt Colin finds it even harder to imagine in his case.

She looks at Colin and sighs. 'Time,' she says, 'for bed.'

'Night-night,' he says, showing no sign of movement other than hand to bottle, glass to mouth.

Oswald arrived early in the morning in a blaze of tweed; all got up for the country. He stepped out of his smart little car, flashed his smart, pearl-toothed smile at her, carefully manoeuvred his smart glistening shoes over the gravel and said, 'Seen you looking worse, Linda.'

Belinda found herself suffused by waves of humiliation. Her first thought was, can a meeting between Oswald and Kenneth be averted?

'You're looking full of beans,' she said, not speaking warmly.

'It's a beautiful morning,' he said, 'and it's great to be back in Scotland. I had breakfast at Gleneagles. It's astonishing the quality you can still get there. I had devilled kidneys and bacon. A kipper first. And really good marmalade. You do yourselves well in Scotland.'

'There are people who don't eat at Gleneagles, I'm told. Silly of them isn't it?'

'I thought I'd come here first, because I've one or two matters I want to discuss with you. Is there anywhere we can go?'

Oswald might welcome the beautiful morning, but it made him uneasy. He wasn't quite sure of his responses out of doors.

'How's Grace?' he said as Belinda led him into a cold sitting-room. 'Did you ever get in touch with Machonie?'

'No,' she said, 'Dr Craig didn't think he could do any good.'

'Ah,' said Oswald, 'well, I guess it's terminal, and when it's terminal there's nothing you can do, it's fatal to think there is. Still it wouldn't have been a bad idea to have had Machonie in. You're always better to consult an expert.'

Having given the absent Machonie this pat on the head, he sat down and crossed his legs.

'I'm sorry she's dying,' he said, 'but she'd had a good life. It's rough for you though, she's been your real mother, hasn't she?'

It was astonishing, how every now and then, the insensitive, crass, and self-centred Oswald could hit a nerve. Once she had found that this couldn't but soften the way she felt, bringing her up against the momentary conviction that she had misjudged him, had allowed social judgement to pose as moral. Now she rather found herself looking for the pay-off. What did he expect in return?

'I'd like to see her,' he said.

She had been thinking about that.

'No,' she said.

Grace hadn't ever liked Oswald. Belinda could remember the pain of her politeness at their first meeting.

'No,' she said again, 'she wouldn't recognize you. She no longer recognizes people. She didn't know Fiona last time she visited, and I'm not having her put on show, that's all. Sorry if it sounds harsh.'

Oswald merely smiled. He had long ago discovered this was a means of getting his way more often than not. If he was refused something, he didn't continue the discussion, he nodded and seemed to accept the decision, smiled, remained amiable and affable, smiled, and then tried to slip the request through on the blind side; alternatively he took 'no' as a satisfactory answer to this question, content in the knowledge that the refusal would make his next bid harder to turn down. He had explained all this to Belinda, at great length. 'You must never lose your temper unless you do so intentionally,' he had said. 'You do much better by seeming to accept. It gets people, that does. They feel flattered and they feel guilty if they think they've got an advantage over you.'

Belinda hadn't been interested. She could never see life as a series of campaigns.

Oswald said, 'Sure, all right then, now you know best, but please convey my regards to her. I had quite an esteem for Grace.'

He couldn't of course bring himself to say, 'even if she didn't think much of me'; but the knowledge hung between them.

'First then,' he said, 'money. I'm selling the flat. Strictly speaking, you're not entitled to anything, since it was mine before we married, but I'm proposing arranging a substantial payment to your account. The only thing is, please don't keep it on current, let it for once earn some money for you. You don't know how much better off you would be if you would just let money work for you.'

'I don't really need this, or want it,' Belinda said. 'You pay me generous alimony as it is.'

But a second voice said, 'if he's giving it as a gesture, it's because he knows that you could extract it by law.'

And, though it might be speaking the truth—Belinda didn't know and could hardly bring herself to be interested—Belinda was ashamed of this voice, as of all those manifestations of the meaner elements that lurk within.

'But the point is,' the flat nasal voice went on, the suburban accent by now ironed out, so that despite the residual nasality, the effect was of something packaged, a mass-market cosmetic or convenience food, 'the point is,' he said, 'you've got to treat what I give you from the flat as capital, not income. That's absolutely imperative, if you don't want to find yourself in a Colin situation. I'm nervous and worried about this, and if there was some way I could see that you couldn't touch it except as working capital, I would. Taxwise I can't. I did think of a trust, but there are complications.'

Belinda felt a quick, pricking irritation. She rubbed her nails on the palm of her hand. Oswald's words conjured up pictures of travel brochures. It was typical of him not to have named the sum. She wondered how long it would serve her at the Hassler in Rome or the Gritti in Venice. That was the effect Oswald had on her. She didn't listen to what he said next, something about an investment trust. It would double her money in a day or two, she gathered. Extraordinary how few people in the country availed themselves of such opportunities. Of course they didn't have the benefit of Oswald's advice. That must be it. He went on. She looked at a picture on the wall, a Victorian oil, done by a great-aunt, she could never remember which. It showed a garden, that, in the picture, looked extensive and park-like. It had probably been something a bit humbler, being the garden of a typical tenant farm in Aberdeenshire, which her great-grandfather had had. Still, there was a seemliness, a decorum about the lawns and hedges, the fine beech trees down one side, and the open fields, themselves called parks in that part of the world, rolling away to blue hills. You could imagine, though they weren't in the picture, cream-coloured tea-gowns brushing the grass. They might be got up by the village dressmaker, from models that appeared in the illustrated press, and the accents of the ladies who wore them might have been by her standards rough (though their grammar would probably, barring any regional peculiarities, have been more certain than Fiona's); nevertheless the painting suggested a style of living, and aspirations beyond it, that she found preferable to listening to Oswald as matter for reflection.

And of course the joke was, they would have been on Oswald's side against Colin and her. The people who lived there could never have treated capital as income. Somehow that wasn't the full equation though.

'Have you thought of anything to do?' said Oswald.

The direct question cut in on her musings.

'I've been fairly occupied,' she said. 'I haven't exactly been thinking of the future.'

'You had several months in Fulham without coming to any decision.'

'Yes.'

'I had hoped that coming up here would have given you the opportunity for some re-orientation and changing direction.'

There was, she told herself, no point in being annoyed by Oswald's assumptions. She had forfeited such right when she first accepted involvement with him. He, after all, hadn't changed. Still she had a horrible vision of Oswald continuing to arrange her life, eventually thrusting her into an Old Folks' Home, for, of course, the best of reasons; her own good, oh God!

'I know something,' she said, 'about your business here, and I can see where you're driving.'

'Good,' he said, 'that gets us into a corner-cutting situation, makes the conversation rather more viable.'

Oswald pursed his lips a moment. 'You've met Gerald, I gather. I'd be very interested to have your impressions.'

Belinda couldn't imagine why. Surely Oswald should have accepted by now that they thought differently about people, as indeed about most everything. It didn't occur to her that Oswald might not be much interested in agreement, that he didn't really seek confirmation of his own view, but rather another angle on it, modification even. He was keen on putting himself in what he called 'a learning situation'.

'He's not quite my cup of tea,' she said.

'There's a dynamic there,' Oswald said, 'I wonder if you think it's under control.'

Belinda shivered a man-walking-on-grave shiver.

'There's something creepy,' she said, 'about his certainty. I can't accept that anyone sane can be that certain.'

'Aren't you perhaps confused by your own capacity for doubt? He's an interesting man, Gerald. What's particularly interesting—and an example of how things come together by different routes, the inter-connectedness of matter—is that from a completely different starting point he's come to the same conclusions as myself, even though we use different language. He talks about hierarchy—that's not my way of putting it—but it's still in line with my thinking.'

Oswald got up, his face a bit flushed. 'I was very interested to hear from him,' he said.

Belinda saw something new in his face. He was like a girl who has at last been asked to dance.

'What exactly are you going to do?' she said.

She didn't want to know, had no possible interest in it, wouldn't believe the answer; yet it was concern that prompted the question. She had made love to Oswald, felt rape in the way Morgan looked at her; you couldn't ignore realities like that.

She expected Oswald not exactly to shy away from an answer, but rather to wrap it up in a smoke-screen of asphyxiating verbiage, so that in the end, though he would doubtless have told her everything that her question seemed to demand, she would have remained ignorant, in the dark, not having been able to bring herself to listen. Instead he surprised her—Morgan's influence?—by a straight answer.

'We're setting up a camp to train trade unionists.'

Belinda almost laughed. That was her first reaction. It was, as so often with what is funny, a matter of simple incongruity. Oswald and trade unionists, they went together like bishops and banana skins. What on earth did he think he was going to train them to do? Jump through hoops?

'Are they going to like that?' she said.

'The thing's imperative,' he said.

Even if she had laughed it wouldn't have mattered. Oswald would merely have continued puffing his pipe, waiting for her laughter to subside, before going ahead with his patient, complacent exposition.

Which he now proceeded to give her.

It appeared that the lines of thinking independently pursued by Morgan and himself had come to meet at this point. Industrial indiscipline and the disinclination to work were certainly, in one sense, at the root of our endemic national weakness. In another sense however they were merely manifestations—'comprehensible and ultimately legitimate manifestations'—of an inadequate because alienating ethos. Accordingly what was needed urgently was a change in ethos, or, put it another simpler way, in attitude of mind. Dignity had to be restored to industrial activity (whatever that meant). This was where Oswald and Morgan came together. Their camps—the one they proposed to set up now was merely the first of a network that would cover the whole of the United Kingdom and probably, Oswald thought but confessed Morgan was doubtful, eventually the EEC. 'Bit of a disagreement here. Gerald retains old imperial attitudes, natural for one who has spent much of his life in an empire-regulating role.' Their camps then would not teach technical skills but would encourage right thinking about society. They would instil an understanding of where people fitted in. That was the thing.

'Sounds a bit like *Arbeit macht frei*,' said Belinda sourly.

'We mustn't allow ourselves to be dominated by stereotypes,' Oswald said, 'that was after all a very good motto. It is true; that's what work does.'

'And how,' she couldn't stop herself from asking, 'are you going to get recruits? It doesn't sound to me the sort of thing you'll find the workers falling over each other to get in a queue for.'

'There'll be incentives,' said Oswald. 'Now, as Morgan put it to you, not very well, I gather, we need an administrative assistant, and it could be you.'

'Not exactly my cup of tea.'

'I think you should think very seriously about it. You know, Linda, there's a lot of us worried about you. You're at a crisis point, and in my opinion this offers you the sort of chance that won't come often to avoid the Colin syndrome.'

She had never found it easy to say 'no' to Oswald, and she couldn't tell why. There had been no difficulty in turning down Morgan, ostensibly a far stronger, more dominating personality. Of course, one thing was that she had no doubt

Morgan was just plain nasty, while she didn't feel like that about Oswald. She looked out of the window.

Colin was standing on the expanse of gravel. He put his hand in his pocket, drew out a cigarette and a lighter, and cupped his hands to light it. Then he walked, dog-like, stiff-legged over to Oswald's car and walked slowly round it, eyes fixed in a steady glare, nose twitching as if in sniffing suspicion—if he had indeed been a dog, there could have been no doubt about it: he was considering which wheel he would urinate against. Then his head jerked up. He looked towards the corner of the drive. Belinda followed his gaze and saw a car, which she had not yet heard, come round the corner. It was a big, old-fashioned Humber, containing no doubt that old-fashioned thing, a caller.

Colin, she was surprised to note, hadn't made off. That meant that he recognized the car and was prepared to encounter its occupant. Astonishing.

The car stopped. The door opened. There was a huge heaving, and Margot Rutherford extricated herself from behind the wheel. Meanwhile the other door opened and a man who was familiar but to whom Belinda couldn't immediately give a name slid out in a rather lizard-like manner, followed abruptly by two leaping and exuberant boxer pups. At whom Margot Rutherford, without greeting Colin, began to roar instructions, which the dogs disregarded.

'Visitors,' said Belinda, 'you'll have to excuse me. Maybe you want to get on anyway.'

'I'm in no hurry,' said Oswald, joining her at the window. 'Why, it's Mansie Niven, I was hoping to meet him.'

And so indeed it was. Balding when Belinda had last seen him perhaps ten years ago, he now wore a fine lustrous wig. That had deceived her. Now that she knew who he was, the slack mouth and darting eyes were recognizably familiar.

'My God,' she said, 'so it is.'

'I wouldn't have come in,' said Margot Rutherford, 'if Mansie hadn't insisted on coming with me. I was just calling

91

to see how poor Grace was, but when Mansie heard you were here, wild horses weren't even also rans, my dear.'

She gave Belinda a smacking kiss.

'You're looking terrible,' she said. 'What's Patrick Craig thinking he's at, letting you wear yourself out like this. Some people would say you needed a tonic, but I'm an old hand at this sort of exhaustion and I recommend champagne. What are you thinking of, Colin, not to give her champagne?'

She positively purred as she spoke to Colin; she was one of his surviving admirers. Belinda remembered he had never been able to do wrong in her eyes.

'And you've got rid of Annie, my dear. I'm delighted to hear it. That woman would fret a cat to death. And cats are no' easy fretted. And who's this?'

She fixed Oswald with a look that seemed to call for a lorgnette.

'You've met Oswald, surely,' said Belinda. 'My ex-husband.'

'Oh yes, I've met him, fair enough, but what's he doing here?'

'He's got some business in Scotland, he just called in.'

'Business, what business, that's what I'd like to know?'

Oswald had contrived to detach Mansie Niven from them —notwithstanding Mansie's expressed enthusiasm for meeting Belinda again—and was talking earnestly to him in the corner. Belinda couldn't catch what he was saying. She guessed he was flattering Mansie and praising himself.

'Poor Grace, has she got long to go?' said Margot.

'Any day, Patrick says.'

'It'll be the end of an era. She and I, we're the last survivors of the old days. I remember fine when Grace and the Major came here, that was when I was married to Billy, still. People sometimes say to me, doesn't it seem like another life when you look back, and do you know what I say, Belinda? I say, it seems like the real one. That stymies them, not that anyone under fifty knows what a stymie is.'

'Oh yes I do.'

'Ah, but you're one of the old school, m' dear. So's Colin.

How you came to marry that counter-jumper and Colin that little tart, I'll never know.'

Margot sat down, her fat squeezing itself into a high-backed chair.

'Lord, Lord,' she said, 'as my sister-in-law, Dorothy, used to say, "there's nowt so queer as folk". I don't like that feller your sister's picked up; a wrong 'un if ever I met one.'

Belinda had never been able to decide whether Margo employed these expressions, which would have been out-of-date even in her girlhood, purely naturally, by the operation of some atavistic sympathy, or whether they were her chosen affectation.

'No,' she said, 'I don't care for him either.'

'Between you and me and the bedpost, m' dear, he's the sort of feller used to be blackballed from clubs, take my word for it. I met one or two of his kidney in my time, specially when in India with Billy. Wrong 'uns every one, no matter what their manner. Not that I like Morgan's. Damned impertinent, I call 'em. You tell your sister, she'll listen to you, has a great respect for you, but just thinks me an old fool, you tell her to get shot of him or she'll regret it. Mind you, you'll have a hard row to hoe, she's besotted. Talking of which, you want to watch your own step, m' girl. I saw you come back that night with young Kenneth. That's the wrong sort of attachment for you, not that it wouldn't do him a power of good, the graceless loon. No, you'd do better with Mansie there, even if he is my nephew.'

'Mansie, your nephew, I'd forgotten that.'

'My only sister's only boy. Mansie's no great shakes, I grant you, but he's an M.P. and that's still something, maybe, and you should have seen his face light up at the prospect of meeting you again.'

'It's years since I met him.'

'Ah, he's a sentimental loon. His father was a fool, he gets the sentiment from that side. Now that,' she said on a changed note, 'is what I call style.'

Belinda looked up. Colin was returning with a tray of glasses and a magnum of Pol-Roger.

'You shouldn't have taken me so literally, m' dear,' Margot said, 'not that you'll hear a grumble.'

Colin looked over his shoulder from the side-table where he was placing the tray. 'Grumble,' he said, 'I should think not.'

He uncorked the bottle with a pop, but without wasting any champagne.

'I can't stand,' Margot said, 'these young idiots who throw half a bottle of wine over the room when they open it. So unnecessary.'

Colin took her a glass, and gave one to Belinda.

'Niven,' he said, 'there's some wine here. Help yourself when you feel like it.' He came over and stood by Margot's chair, sipping.

'Lucy Longlegs in the 3.30 at Sandown,' he said.

'Do you think she'll stay?' said Margot.

'She's bred to.'

'You can't rely on breeding nowadays, specially where fillies are concerned. Pep pills and stimulants . . .'

'Oh there's decadence and corruption there too,' said Colin.

'It's everywhere, it's a disease.'

'Well, Belinda,' said Mansie Niven, who having scurried over for his wine, showed no desire to return to Oswald, now abandoned in the window-recess. 'Well, Belinda, a lot of water under many bridges . . .'

'Oh yes, I suppose so.'

She wondered if she should mention the wig.

'I didn't recognize you for a moment.'

'It must be ten years at least.'

'Oh how aging life is,' she said.

'It was at the Fife Hunt Ball we last met.'

She sighed. The dances of youth had receded into a mist. She couldn't even remember all her dresses, let alone her partners.

'I thought you married Susie Rayne,' she said.

'That's right. It didn't last. It's difficult being an M.P.'s wife, of course, Susie didn't like it.'

94

'Any children?'

'Two boys.'

'Well, that's nice. Look,' she said, 'you'll have to excuse me for a moment, I've just got to run upstairs and see how Grace is. You have some more wine and talk to Oswald. He's very eager to involve you in a scheme of his.'

'And fascinating it sounds too.'

Mansie had a way of wiggling his Adam's apple whenever he spoke with enthusiasm. He did this now and she saw him as real for the first time.

He also nodded briskly. 'I'm sorry though you have to rush; poor Grace, you must give her my love, she's a pillar of the county.'

'Oh no,' said Belinda, 'not that, and she's past receiving anyone's expression of love, poor dear. She's on the way out and she's almost there.'

She went out into the hall and felt a chill. There was actually no point in going up to see Grace. She had been in a deep sleep earlier, the nurse was with her, Belinda could only be a nuisance; the nurse was replacing her as she had supplanted Annie. Instead she went outside. It had started to rain. This surprised her. There had been no hint of cloud earlier. It must have come up quickly from behind the hills. She came in and went towards the kitchen. A banging of pots suggested Annie might be there. It was better to avoid her. She went into the small sitting-room, and looked at the case of stuffed birds; you could read concentration and worry on the face of the Malayan Robin. She lit a cigarette and stood by the window while she smoked it in quick puffs.

She could, of course, telephone.

If Fiona answers think of some other excuse.

If it's Gavin, ask to speak to Fiona.

'Thank goodness it's you, I hadn't been able to think of what I would have said if it had been Fiona.'

'. . . . .'

95

'I don't seem to have seen you for ages . . .'

'. . . . . . .'

'I came over yesterday, but you weren't about, not that I blame you for that.'

'. . . . .'

'Why don't you . . . ?'

'. . . . .'

'This afternoon?'

'. . . . .'

'I am looking forward to . . . listen, there are some people here now, but I don't think they'll stay much longer . . . about three o'clock, no, I don't suppose we'll do anything, but . . .'

'. . . . .'

'But . . .'

Receivers are replaced. They click simultaneously. A faint humming is almost certainly imaginary, but it is the imagination working truly. There is, indeed, a faint, sympathetic hum. How does he feel? Is there any quickening of the heartbeat? She puts her fingers on hers. The rhythm is certainly strong, almost certainly faster than normal. But perhaps all he feels is that it is a way of getting through the day.

She doesn't think it's like that. His voice didn't suggest it was like that. There was a nervousness in its timbre.

But was it merely that he was afraid he would be found at the telephone, asked who he was speaking to, and consequently embarrassed for an answer?

She mounts the stair to her room. The light wavers and changes as she turns the corner of the stair, passing the roses in their vase.

It is absurd to imagine that he might feel as she does.

He is eighteen and she is thirty-five.

But back in her bedroom, which is a place where emotions can almost be confessed, where the defences are down every morning as she sits before her dressing table, her clothes feel slightly damp and she decides to change. Her skin is hot and moist. She lies on the bed a moment, wrapped in a towel. Her eyes move to the picture and the expression in the eyes of the shepherdesses suggests the picture is another mirror. She lies back with her head against the pillows, her body snuggled in the cocoon of the thick towel, and her left hand comes across to hug her right shoulder, pressing hard. The hand disappears in blonde hair as she pushes her head down on to it.

A car drives away. She hopes it is Oswald. She falls asleep.

It was in fact Margot Rutherford and Mansie who had departed, leaving Oswald standing in the bow window looking out. Colin, turning away from Margot's car, saw him still standing there and scuffed his toe at a stone. He hunched his shoulders and looked down at the gravel. He dug his hands deep in his trouser pockets (old-fashioned pockets at the side). He didn't know whether Oswald was watching him or not.

On the other hand there was still wine in the bottle.

He went back to the morning-room and poured a glass and was on the point of leaving with it, when he was arrested by Oswald's voice.

'Do you know where Linda's got to?'

'No.'

'It's irritating, I've got to get on, but . . .'

'Then why don't you?'

Colin raised his head as he said this. Catching sight of it in the glass, pushed back on his shoulders, he saw it as a failed Roman Emperor's head. Tiberius gazing at the Fariglioni blackly splitting the deep blue ocean from the deep blue sky, and unable in the profound heat of a Capri afternoon to contemplate exertion, even for the sort of orgy with which the ignorant peasantry and ignorant and malicious senators in thievish scandal-mongering Rome a world away idly credited him; or Nero wishing the human race had but a single neck; but not alas Hadrian, in villaed and many fountained Tivoli, with the Sabine landscape perfectly formed and poised below him and around him, the well-ordered vines, the olive groves, the crops, 'the large contented oxen heaving slow'; never Hadrian.

'Why don't you,' he said, head still thrown back, 'simply bugger off?'

For a moment it looked as if Oswald would just obey, swallow his dignity, and allow himself to be ejected thus unceremoniously. He even advanced two or three steps towards the door, while Colin held his gaze. Then he stopped and said, 'I almost forgot. I saw Julie the other day. She was very interested when I told her I was coming up, and asked me to give you this.' He fished in his briefcase. 'She said it was yours.' He produced a small leather bag and handed it to Colin.

Colin knew at once what was in it, even though he hadn't been aware that it wasn't already in his possession. It was a small amulet, made of copper. They had found it in an ironworker's shop in Acri in Calabria. It was not so much the subject—a fish—that had attracted Julie as the place where they had found it, for she had somehow learned that Acri was where the inhabitants of ancient Sybaris had banished their smiths that they might not be distressed by the sound of labour. It was an extraordinary piece of information for Julie to have acquired. And what did she mean by it now?

'Well, well,' he said, 'very funny.'

'I don't know if you've seen Julie recently,' Oswald said. He sat down on the arm of a chair. 'She's not looking as she used to look. I'd say she's in considerable difficulties. To my way of thinking, sending you this was a cry for help.'

Colin drew the little amulet out from the leather case. The fish arched its back sinuously and the anchor which passed behind it made another arching back.

'You know the inarticulacy that so easily affects people in Julie's situation. It sounded to me as if by sending you this Julie was calling out to you. I take it it's a reminder of something, a souvenir or memory. She was a bit drunk when she gave it to me. There was no sudden impulse however. She actually called me up. She'd met someone who'd told her I was coming to Scotland, and she called me up and said she wanted to meet me. We arranged to meet in a pub. I didn't much care for it, the Queen's Elm it's called, I expect you know it. Well, she was already, had already obviously had several drinks before I arrived. She cried a bit when she talked about you, with great affection if I may say so. And she gave me this, said you would be sure to know what she meant by it . . .'

He paused, waiting for Colin to tell him.

The shop in Acri had been a subterranean cavern in a sour-smelling side-street. They'd emerged from a wine-shop more or less next door, where they'd spent the afternoon hours drinking a heavy black wine of the locality and eating bread and olives and salami and one of those Calabrian cheeses with a knob of butter contained in them. The two or three black-suited and black-hatted locals, who had also been in the wine-shop, playing *scopa*, had frowned at Julie. They hadn't liked seeing her there. Acri wasn't a town that had been at all infected by tourism; wine-shops were for men. Even Julie, not the most sensitive to atmosphere, had been aware of it. It had perhaps encouraged her to drink a little more, and they had stayed there through the siesta, finding it too hot to move back to their anyway unattractive hotel room, as they'd originally intended. At last, the proprietress of the wine-shop, goitred and black-clad, had come to their table to speak to them, having decided after two or three hours that they were '*gentili e signorili*'. They'd found her dialect almost impenetrable, as she discoursed of the glories and brutality of Acri. It seemed one moment to be *Paradiso*; the next *l'Inferno*. But it was of course from her they'd learned its reputed fabulous origin.

So, Julie, giggling and wine-drugged, had determined she must buy Colin a memento of this most appropriate of places.

And here, again, it was.

It certainly wasn't modern.

Reluctantly, Oswald at last decided that he wasn't going to learn anything from Colin. He glanced at his watch, was visibly affected by what he saw. He picked up the briefcase.

'I'm being serious,' he said, 'when I say she was asking for help. I don't think you should ignore it. I'm sorry Linda seems to have vanished, but I appreciate that she thinks Grace must come first just now. Tell her, will you, I'll ring this evening. She's really got to decide what's best for her to do.'

Colin gave a little grunt.

Belinda woke feeling guilty. This wasn't unusual. Once, she would have said, guilt passed her by. She could have described herself as 'blithe'; like a milkmaid. Not any more.

Also she had a headache and felt a little sick. That wasn't so bad. The guilt might simply be a manifestation of some physical disorder; only nothing was that simple.

Grace might have died.

Her dream had made her guilt. She couldn't summon it up clearly, and, attempting, almost lost what she had. Kenneth had been sitting (reclining surely? he couldn't have been sitting upright) in a great bare classical courtyard; a landscape with columns. She had approached him from behind, in sandalled feet, over the baking and uneven pavement. She had startled lizards. There were no birds in the blue sky, but she could hear the crickets' remorseless unending chirk. From the courtyard, which was open on that side, the ground had fallen abruptly away, first dark-green, then into a black chasm, towards, she could sense, a lake of pitch; it was in that direction that she was walking. She placed her hand on Kenneth's right shoulder, which was bare of the tunic, and then moved it lightly up to adjust/take off the laurel wreath that crowned his brow. He looked up with long-lipped smile. A sound of metal distracted her. She glanced across. In the far corner of the courtyard, a violet-robed priest was sharpening a knife or sickle. He stood at an altar. He gave a harsh cry and two other men, acolytes perhaps, for they were no more than youths, approached dragging a kid. A cloud dipped over the sun, Belinda shivered and awoke, guilty and trembling.

She got off the bed, swinging her bare feet to the ground, and padded across the room, poured herself a glass of water and drank it. How good it was.

She looked at her watch; a quarter to three. What of Nurse's lunch? But, if Grace had died, they would have woken her.

'I had almost decided to give you up and go in again. It's terrible I went to sleep and the nurse missed her lunch. She's been very nice about it, but I felt awful. Lunch is important to people like nurses. So I took her sandwiches and a chicken salad and cheese and pickles, she's very fond of pickles, and said I was too terribly sorry but I had someone coming to see me, and did she mind. She said Grace was no trouble, poor lamb she's never been any since I've arrived, and was it my young man was coming? God knows what she meant by that, or imagined. Mind you, she'd be pleased to think you were, because she's obviously fallen for Patrick Craig and she's afraid I might have made a click with him . . . I had such a funny dream . . . you were in it . . . I woke up before it turned nasty but I felt nasty when I woke up . . . you're looking very pretty today, of course afternoon boredom is very sexy, and long fingers and long lips . . . shall we walk to the sun-dial, there's something about sun-dials . . . watching the creeping shadow marks time so much more convincingly, so much more movingly, than the passage of the clock's hands . . . Grace will have gone this time next week . . . shall I remain . . . we will have to get through all the agony, the contest with and to the death, the family reunion, the complications, the little battles of personality, my mother, my brother . . . I shall need you to keep me me . . .'

Some of this, but not much, Belinda says as she and Kenneth walk through the woods of beech and chestnut, laurel, birch and oak, to a large clearing where, sometime in the nineteenth century, a summer-house had been built of rustic timber, and, incongruously, a sun-dial set up on its little pedestal.

The trouble is, she can't really think of what to say. If she talks of what is uppermost in her mind, he will shy away, like a young deer. If she tells him stories from her fabulous past, stories which would fit her present mood better than he could possibly appreciate, that will be no good either; they might not frighten him; they couldn't fail to remind him that his much older brother is married to her much younger sister. She can't talk of Grace. She can't ask him about his plans.

He doesn't, she is quite certain, want to talk about what he hasn't got, only vague disinclinations; and he almost certainly has more of that than he can stomach from Fiona and Gavin. 'You've got to come to a decision, you know. Your whole future depends on it. There are already enough frightful examples of drifting in the family . . .' Oh God, oh God, no doubt it's like that, quite sufficiently like that . . . There is always her visit from Oswald, and though she is ashamed of Oswald and doesn't like the idea of Kenneth thinking of her in relationship to Oswald, still there is the story of the job and the Oswald–Morgan Camp for the Rehabilitation and Right-Thinking of Trade Unionists. It is after all a comic turn and so right down their street.

'I had a visit from my ex-husband this morning,' she says.

'I think all that sort of thing's terribly boring,' he says.

'What?' She is surprised.

'Husbands, ex-husbands, wives, ex-wives, I never want to go in for it. Why . . . not, you understand, Belinda, that I want to go in for the other thing either, like your brother Andrew . . .'

'Andrew, what do you know about Andrew . . . my dear?' she daringly adds.

'I met Andrew in London, just by chance, I was passing through on my way back to Eton from Cambridge. He took me for a drink in a pub. It was obvious what sort of pub it was. He was trying me out, I think.'

'And . . . ?'

'One of his friends put his hand on my shoulder and squeezed. No, don't laugh, I know it doesn't sound much but it was . . . it made me shiver.'

And, she doesn't say, If I put my hand on your shoulder and squeeze, what sort of shiver would there be . . . ?

'Why can't we all just live in compartments, leave each other alone?'

They have come to the sun-dial. The grove however is by now in shadow. Anyway, since it was built, the trees have grown, their branches spread, and in the summer, only at noon, when the sun casts no shadow, does the clearing receive

its rays. In the winter they slant through the bare branches,
make the shadow line waver and hard to read.

> *e la lor cieca vita e tanto bassa*
> *che invidiosi son d'ogni altra sorte*

The words come into Belinda's mind from the chief of the
poets she ever reads now (others are Swinburne, Eliot and
Dylan Thomas).

She knows she has every sympathy with what Kenneth
says. It is just what she wants herself, only just at the
moment she wants Kenneth too.

'It's terrible,' she says, 'how you stumble into things. I
never meant to marry Oswald, you know. It just became
easier to do that than not to. Does that sound terribly feeble?'

Kenneth doesn't reply to this. He is scratching at the moss
on the base of the sun-dial, scratching not very effectively
with long pale forefinger.

'It's Latin,' he says at last, 'do you know Latin? It's the
only subject that ever seemed worth doing to me, they didn't
let me do Greek, I can't remember why, some nonsense of
my father's, but Latin made sense.'

'Have you been to Italy?'

'Florence, I didn't care for it, we have cousins there and
we stayed with them.'

Belinda sits down. 'Florence,' she says, 'is a test. If you
like Florence, at any rate if it's your favourite Italian city, you
don't really like Italy. You may even dislike it. Oddly, that's
not true of Venice, which is a museum too, but then I always
think Venice isn't really Italy, it's just Venice. But liking
Florence best, well Florence is like Edinburgh, don't you
think, and the sort of cousins people have in Florence have
something in common with Morningside.'

'I don't know anything about Morningside, I don't even
know where it is.'

'It's a Victorian suburb of Edinburgh, very correct.'

'Oh, well correct's what you could call my cousins in
Florence. You've lived in Italy, haven't you?'

'Yes.'

'Are you going to go back there?'

She pauses. This is what she recognizes as the great temptation. She hasn't been admitting it, but now the question is in the open, lying there, like an orange on a white plate, unmistakable, undeniable.

'If I do,' she says at last, 'you must come to stay with me.'

It is out, or it is almost out, but Kenneth doesn't seem to have noticed. Instead he gets up, perhaps that means he notices, and goes, light-footed, to the edge of the clearing, and looks long down the winding path by which they approached it.

'Thought I heard someone,' he says, at last, 'perhaps I didn't . . .'

III

Colin and Belinda in the kitchen.

Colin in his accustomed place, bottle and glass to hand, but turning over, over and over again, the amulet Julie has sent him.

'Your ex-husband,' he says, 'doesn't improve, nor does your ex-admirer Niven.'

Belinda turns from her task, which is the filling of a coffee-pot, 'Not so ex-Mansie,' she says, 'he fancies me still.'

'Do you find that reassuring?'

'Not particularly. What's that you're fiddling with?'

He holds it up so that she can see the leaping fish.

'Where did it come from?'

'My ex-wife sent it by way of your ex-husband. Does that sound like a conspiracy?'

'Why can't they both leave us alone?'

She puts the coffee on the Aga and sits at the table to wait, resting her chin in her hands. She looks at her brother through tired and narrowed eyes. His own are opaque or glazed, with no suggestion of feeling.

'Of course they can't leave us alone,' he says. 'They are obsessed by us, didn't you know that?'

'It's never struck me quite like that.'

'Well, let it do so.'

'I thought to be quite honest, that is, I've often thought recently, wondering why things went wrong for both of us, that we rather fed off them. Oswald and Julie have energy. You can't claim that for either of us.'

He pours himself a glass of his red wine, which calls itself *vin du pays* but which probably owes more to factory workers than to peasants.

'Of course I don't. That's not the point . . .'

She is not going to admit it to Colin, and she hardly likes to confess it to herself, but she can see that he is in a way right. Only she doesn't know what has prompted him to come to this.

'We kept them up to the mark,' says Colin.

She seeks irony in what he has said. The search is vain. On Colin's grey cheek she sees the tremor of a nerve.

'Julie's a little slut,' he says. 'Just what Margot Rutherford calls her, a little tart. I didn't let her get away with that sort of behaviour.'

Belinda can think of many occasions, all too many, when she herself knew of Julie's adulteries. There was that black actor who played in *Puss in Boots* with her, the young American in the TV version of *The Ill-Made Knight* (an American Lancelot because it had been essential to sell it to the States, though they had actually failed to do so, thus scoring a left and right, a commercial and critical botch), the aging Tom Bristow, one of the few surviving poets of the Apocalyptic Movement not to have recanted; and so on and so on; these were merely the ones that leapt to Belinda's mind. And also the picture of Julie hugging her knees and saying, 'Colin's gone off bodies altogether, you know. Sometimes I wonder if a spot of necrophilia mightn't manage to arouse him, but I can't think of anything else that could.'

'She's obviously going to pieces on her own,' Colin says.

'And are you going to pick them up?'

He gives her a blank boiled-cod stare.

'If I were you,' he says, 'I would make it pretty clear to Oswald that there's nothing doing. I would tell him to fuck off, if I were you. He's a limpet. You'll have him stuck to you for life if you don't watch out.'

It is much later than usual. Belinda drinks coffee. There is a long cobwebbed silence as they sit there, Belinda aware of Colin as a presence with a certain surprising moral weight, even if this is only conveyed by apathy, lack of enthusiasm, disillusion and disapproval. He is going away from her, excluding even her, because though in so many ways, yes her heart still beats with his, there are limits. It is often against what she would like to feel, and even when she assents to Colin and says 'it is not just prejudice, it reflects, oh faintly and distortedly, a standard that has indeed some of the superiority he incongruously claims,' there is always a part that says also, 'No'; for it is a narrowing alley he travels down, and she can see no exit for him.

Through the night the owl hoots, warning off others, warning also, one would think, its prey. Colin's bottle is empty. He pulls himself to wavering heavy feet, and with the portentous deliberation that is the mark of his condition, manoeuvres round the table's edge, negotiates the skirting of the dresser, fishes in the big cardboard box and extracts another litre. There is a profundity about the whole proceeding; it is the grand business, and when it is done, the glass re-filled, air is filled with the hum of triumph, all tension relaxes; world is, in a sense, seen to be good. Belinda consents to live the lie, step out of nature. She pushes her coffee cup aside and says, 'I might have some of your muck too.'

Does it offer, far from nectar though it be, gold imaginings?

Belinda would like to go back, to try out Colin's memories and ask him when he last looked forward to next week, even to the waking day. Yet oddly he is not unhappy. Self-content is clear enough. And she herself is not unhappy, and in imagination draws her finger across Kenneth's lips.

The wine is nasty enough, but not so bad if you swig deep.

There comes a rap at the window. The door leading to the yard (a door which is never locked, for there is no point in locking doors here in this house, where windows yield to finger pressure, so that eventually even Annie has come to desist—anyway Grace's front door has only ever been closed when she has been away and the house shut up), the door leading to the yard then is heard to open, and the sound of laughter is admitted. Belinda, startled, looks at Colin. He has not budged. She wonders whether it is some of his drinking chums, yokels from the Graham Arms, come to sponge on him. She has heard Annie complain of this, offended. It is the sort of thing that Grace wouldn't like either; even her easy tolerance would jib here . . .

She hasn't known of such an occasion this time, but once last year, she had come down to the kitchen to find Colin entertaining the local garage proprietor, the rat-catcher and two farm labourers.

But it is in fact Martin and Patrick Craig, and she can see at once that they have been drinking long and deep. No doubt the Graham Arms has played a part in their night.

From Martin's right hand dangles a bottle of Glenmorangie from which two or three drinks, possibly swigs straight from the bottle, have been taken. The neck of a second bottle protrudes from the capacious poacher's pocket of his Norfolk jacket. The jacket itself, a dull Lovat mixture, hangs open, unbuttoned and unbelted. Belinda can see that Martin's trousers were bought for a fatter man. Even though they are belted tight so that little tucks appear, they sag behind and at the hips. He sits down heavily beside her.

'We've not been exactly celebrating,' he says, 'merely drinking deep, having discovered a coincidence of mood. Then we dived deeper into the mood, reached a point when we thought of you but we have not yet descended to Colin's level. Does that make sense to you?'

At this time of night Belinda has no difficulty in making sense of any speech where she can recognize these accents.

'Colin, you old bugger,' says Martin, 'put away your rot-gut and have a proper drink.'

Colin pushes an unfinished glass of red aside and says, 'Craig, you're still on your feet, you'll find glasses over there and water in the tap.'

'I like this kitchen,' says Patrick Craig, when he has given them all whiskies large enough, Belinda thinks, to make it unnecessary for him to replenish the glasses for a bit to come. Indeed there is not much left in the first bottle. Only a certain native caution, bred to believe that 'it's aye wise tae keep a bitty back', has prevented Patrick from dividing the bottle between the four tumblers, which are admittedly large ones.

'It has a pleasant air,' he says.

'You see a broken man,' says Martin. 'Your friend Mansie

has scored a triumph at a public meeting tonight. His career is assured.'

'How did he come to do that?'

'With a speech proposing the establishment of Labour Camps, apparently. I wasn't there, so don't know the details, but it went down a treat, they were even talking about it in the Graham Arms. So there was nothing to do but get, what you see me, drunk. For which I apologise.'

'Never explain, never apologise,' says Colin. 'Secret of my success in life.'

'If we all had a success like you, Colin, the world would be a quieter place.'

Patrick Craig says, 'It's all a charade anyway.'

If only that were true. It is of course a charade but the realities it masks are several, and not just the urgent reality of the private life.

'So what do you do,' Colin says, 'emigrate? Is it 1933 all over again? Are you going to be a good German, Martin?'

'I farm 800 acres.'

'If you admit,' says Colin, 'that we have improved on the Biblical three score years and ten, then between us we just about hit that point *nel mezzo del cammin di nostra vita. Che bella figura faciamo tutti.*'

'It's terrible,' says Patrick Craig, quietly and to Belinda, but his words nevertheless falling into the little pool of silence Colin has summoned up, 'a doctor getting in the state I'm in. It's not as if I'm not on call, it's dereliction of duty, but it happens sometimes. Let's hope the nurse doesn't come down.'

'Oh no,' Belinda says, 'she'll be asleep, and Grace is sleeping soundly too, I looked in before I came down to the kitchen.'

'But,' says Patrick Craig, 'we're not just technicians.'

'*Che bella figura,*' Colin repeats. 'Look at us all. I am, I confess, unemployable, and that may be to my credit in the world we live in. So of course is Belinda, though she manages to hide it better. And you two are of course by contrast pillars of the community.' He drinks some whisky. Perhaps the whisky is working quickly on top of the wine; it is anyway evident that he is going to unburden himself of something. 'But look at our records, our matrimonial records. Belinda marries a vulgar pushing idiot. Why? Because he says he's going to marry her? She can't stand the sight of him and goes on seeing him.'

Belinda looks down at her fingers cradling themselves round the tumbler. There is no point interrupting Colin.

'I marry a little whore, whom I can't keep off the streets and now that she's sinking she looks round for a helping hand,' He turns the amulet over on the table to his right. 'Do I give her that hand or the boot in the face she deserves? I do neither; just sit waiting for Grace to die. Martin hates his wife and is afraid to tell her what she already knows and doesn't even have the guts to leave her.'

'Steady, Colin.'

'Craig of course is different. He's a doctor, a servant of the community. All he does is drive his wife into the bin. We're a great lot and a credit to our rank and nation.'

Colin throws his head back and begins to sing,

'Three naked men be we,
Underneath the hangman's tree
Naked dingle-dangle see
Malefactors swinging free . . .'

'And look at Belinda too,' he says now, 'cradle-snatching.'

Belinda though has been keeping her eyes on Patrick Craig's face, which is set tight and unrevealing; yet it is obviously true what Colin has said. The missing piece of the jigsaw has been provided. She wonders how you take steps to prove your love is mad.

'That's enough, Colin,' Martin says.

'You don't like it, eh?'

'You've said too much.'

'It's the way we live, that's all, let's have it out in the open, cards on the jolly old table. Come on, Martin, what do you hope for from the next five years, ten, twenty, let them stretch on till . . . even your pathetic politics have let you down. Do you know what we are, we're dinosaurs.'

'Maybe there's something in what you say.' Patrick Craig

is speaking in a tone which has all the level reasonableness of a dam that is still doing its job, 'we'd be fools to pretend there isn't. Possibly I'd rather you hadn't mentioned Kathy, it's not something I talk about, or I'd have told you, Belinda, perhaps I should have told you anyway, but believe me I would if it had ever come to the point when it would have been unfair not to . . . I'm getting lost. Let me start again.'

He pauses, wrinkles his brow, while Colin, a bit flushed, lurches to his feet, grabs the whisky bottle by the neck and slops the last of it into his own tumbler, which he brings to his lips, just as he subsides heavily into his chair. And it is a miracle that, drunk like that, the whisky doesn't set off a coughing fit.

'But you make too much of it. There are all sorts of things make marriage difficult today. Believe me, as a doctor I see plenty examples. It may be that it's simply no longer a state that corresponds satisfactorily to other forces in our society that pull in other directions, but I'm not so drunk that I don't know I'm entering deep waters there. But the thing is this, there's a certain coincidence in our situations but I'm damned if I see much similarity in the way we've reached them. Kathy went mad. Nobody knows just why. There's strong reason to believe though that it was a physical condition, and an inherited one. Bad luck on her, bad luck on me. I know about Martin's situation, I know he'd rather I didn't talk about it, but since you're being so dramatic, I'll just say this. It's easy for marriages to go sour, and there's more room for the woman to change within marriage than there used to be. As for you and Belinda, well that just sounds like two cases of original incompatibility.'

'How simple you make it sound,' says Colin who has clearly not listened to any of it.

'Oh, fuck off, Colin,' Martin says.

'Striking a few attitudes, brother, aren't you?' Belinda says. Martin is glowering and it will be better if a lighter note can be introduced.

'Or stripping them off,' Colin says. 'Dinosaurs and dodos, we'd be that anywhere, but it's even worse when we have a stake in a piddling place like this. Oh yes, I was brought up to despise nationality, except the British cardboard J. Arthur Rank variety. If we're not absentee landlords, it's only because we can't afford to be absent from the land we don't have; if we had it, of course we could be absent from it.'

'But I have 800 acres.'

'Not near enough for absence. Nevertheless within this society (if it exists) there's no place for us, though I s'pose I could do a good quisling.'

'I don't know what you're talking about.'

'Neither,' says Colin, 'do I.'

'But,' Martin continues, 'I know well enough why you're talking. It's another of your bloody smoke-screens, Colin. You've made a muck of things and you look for something outside yourself to explain it. And to make it more convincing you want to involve us all in it. But we're not playing. Our life's oor ba' and you're nae haein' it, so there.'

'Not even the odd kick?' Colin asks, opening his eyes wide and innocent. 'If there's nothing in what I'm saying, then why the hell are we all so drunk?'

'Oh drunk,' says Patrick Craig, 'you've got to get drunk now and then, and if we're not careful the way this conversation's going, we'll all talk ourselves sober.'

As if to reduce the risk he takes a deep swig from his glass. Belinda has barely touched hers yet, and she is not pleased by Patrick's benevolent intervention. She wants it to continue between Colin and Martin. At any moment they may stumble into something significant to her. After all, it's only when you are going into this sort of alcoholic haze that you can discern habitual miasmas.

'Look, ducky,' says Colin, 'at our education. I don't know about Craig's, but I do remember the odd bit about ours, don't you? We were to be the leaders of the nation. Officers and other ranks, wasn't it. Only nobody remembered to tell the other ranks. That was one side of it, the moral side. But what about the other side, the subjects they taught us. The full man, that was the goal wasn't it? Always a place for the Classical specialist, he can turn his hand to anything, they're crying out for classicists in industry, only you won't of course go into industry unless you're thick as two short planks. It's amazing. Absolutely amazing. Of course I'm always finding people baying at the moon for classicists, lunatics they're called. Leadership and Thermopylae, that's what it was all about, with the Symposium thrown in, if you were really bright like me.'

'You know, Colin,' Belinda says, 'you're beginning to sound as if you wished you had become Prime Minister at twenty-four.'

'Not a whit,' Colin says, 'all I want is out of it. The whole pot stinks. What do we have now? You like the modern world? Martin? You think it measures up?'

But it is all too easy, because there are of course plenty of people who have the same sort of education as Colin and who are, in the most conventional terms, successes. They are also far more products of the system than Colin was. He didn't after all like it, was a tiresome rebel and mocker at Public School spirit. No, it is too easy to suggest that golden worlds have turned to dust.

'The hell with it,' says Martin, 'you just find it easier to wallow in mud than wash yourself.'

'A metaphor I find baffling.'

'All right then,' says Martin, 'without metaphors.'

'Without metaphors,' Martin repeats, 'you're pig-idle, Colin. You just don't like work, you don't like other people, you can't be bothered with any of the social accommodations we've all got to make time and time again, and the result is, you've become a bore. I know what you're going to say every bloody time before you open your mouth. You're in a vicious circle that's turning into a whirlpool. It's only your fucking incomprehensible conceit keeps your head above water, just. But for anyone else you're useless.'

'What an indictment,' Colin says. 'And what would you suggest I do about it? Join the Marines?'

'No, though the way you talk, I'm surprised you're not like Fiona, sniffing round that bloody Morgan's boots.'

'Come off it, Martin,' says Belinda. 'Colin and Gerald Morgan, no, the idea's too silly.'

'O.K.,' Martin says, 'sorry I seem to have blown my top.'

He fishes into his pocket for the second bottle, breaks the seal and pours drinks.

'Peace offering,' he says.

'Were we at war?' Colin asks. 'Must have missed the declaration.'

'You're out of date,' Patrick Craig says, 'nobody declares war now, they get into confrontations in the course of on-going peace-keeping situations.'

'And of course,' Martin says, in an afterthought he seemingly can't resist, 'you've no bloody ambitions, can't live without ambitions.'

This is clearly from the heart. Possibly Martin has ambitions for his children, which Belinda knows to be the most destructive of all. Possibly he simply wants to breed a good bull.

'Have you ambitions?' she says to Patrick Craig.

'I ought to have the ambition to get a bit of sleep.'

'Oh, sleep.'

'Having difficulty?'

'Oh I take pills from time to time.'

The tension has relaxed, the night drifts on, Colin tells a long story about Edward VII, perhaps it is about Edward VII anyway, Martin gives a biographical sketch of Mansie Niven, which makes Belinda laugh and would have Mansie on the telephone to his lawyers. Colin passes out.

'Look at him,' Martin says, 'the winner of the Gladstone Memorial Homer Prize.'

They drink a bit more, conversation is like lights on the motorway on a misty night. Martin slides back, his mouth open. Patrick Craig removes the cigarette from Martin's fingers before it can burn itself out against the flesh.

'He's worn out,' he says, 'he needs to get away a bit, he's living on his nerves.'

'What did Colin mean, babysnatching?' he says.

'A joke, nothing but a joke.'

'I hoped that was all. You wouldn't pin your heart on a butterfly.'

'Do you want more whisky?'

'No I've had enough.'

'So've I, but . . . I don't often drink whisky, I have long spells I don't like it, not so much the taste, just the whole feeling that emanates from whisky-drinking—in Scotland, anyway. Gin's really my drink, nice and neutral gin-and-tonic, nobody can reproach you ever for gin-and-tonic.'

They dwindle into silence. It comes to Belinda that they are thinking the same thought. If either said, he to her, she to him, come, let's go to bed, the other would nod, and, with no falling into each other's arms or anything movie-like, they would mount the stairs to her cool dark bedroom, silently undress and get between the sheets, and make efficient, tender, therapeutic love; and that each is waiting for the other to say 'this is what I want'. If she could be certain it would stop at that, if she could be certain there would be no follow-up, no consequences, but that is silly. Certainty of that sort is what you can never have. And she would have to turn to the wall the picture of the shepherdesses and the boy leaning against the Corinthian column.

In the end it is a relief when the window is seen to grey as, with the first birdsong, morning creeps up on them, and she now knows that neither will ever say, 'come, let's to bed'.

That is not their sort of relationship; and it is probably better; yet it cannot be unmixed relief. There is always after all the possibility that what wouldn't have ended there with that single act in her bedroom, would have been a change in direction.

She walks out to the car with him. There is a shiver in the air.

'Takes you back a night like that,' he says, 'you find yourself re-living ways of thinking and feeling you had forgotten. I'll be over to see Grace later in the day. Now a wee sleep, then a bath, then breakfast. What hell life is, but I wouldn't change it for death somehow.'

And, she reflects, that is something that most of them also

115

should admit. His car drives off in the usual direction, without a waver. It is probably best that they should have kept out of each other's harms. Back in the bedroom she sees a smile on the face under the acanthus leaves, a long sly approving smile, that hasn't of course ever been visible there before.

She hasn't slept long, and is awake again. Colin is standing, still fully dressed, by her bedside.

'Look at this,' he says, 'I thought you should be wakened to see it.'

He holds up his hand from which dangles the peacock's body.

'I went for a little stroll, welcome the day, and stumbled over it.'

'A fox,' she says.

'No marks of violence. Natural death, or, in other words, cause of death unknown. Startling to come upon, though. Thought you ought to see it.'

She pulls herself up. The small vicious head and the bright eye swing within easy reach.

'I can't remember when it wasn't here, but I've no idea how long peacocks live.'

'Oh, years and years, there used to be others though, remember?'

'Of course. What are you going to do with it?'

'Put it in Annie's bed, I thought.'

'You couldn't.'

'Couldn't I?'

'What have you done to your face?' she says, noticing.

He puts his hand up to his cheek where the skin is raw and broken. There is a trail of bloodstains runs down to his jawbone.

'Did you fall over something?'

'Not exactly,' he grins with the other side of his face. 'That was Martin.'

'Martin?'

'Yes, he clouted me one. Martin still packs quite a punch, all that wrestling with bulls I expect.'

'But why on earth?'

'I suggested to him he'd be better not to drive. This is what happens when I do what everybody says I should do, act the good citizen. Martin has this curious affliction, you know, unless he sleeps twelve, fourteen hours he wakes up drunker than he passed out. Something metabolic. So he was lurching all over the place and I told him he'd be a fool to drive and he landed me one.'

'But is he all right?'

'Well he missed the gatepost, I followed him up the drive to make sure. It was on the way back I fell over Sadie here.'

'It wasn't Martin, was it? Killed it, I mean. Hit it with the car?'

'No, but I don't mind saying it was, he's been a little tiresome, Martin.'

'Well,' sighs Belinda, 'I'm glad you showed me, but now I'd like to have another little snooze, whisky doesn't agree with me.'

'You should take a firmer line with your insides, it's all a matter of will. I suppose I'd better bury Sadie. Say nothing to Grace about it, she was fond of the brute.'

'Of course not, as if I would.'

'On the other hand,' says Colin, holding the bird up, now in both hands, 'perhaps not. I think I'll have the old chap stuffed. There's an excellent taxidermist in Perth. Think I might toddle in there straightaway, I've no idea of the timing of these matters, how quick it's got to be done.'

'That's a brilliant scheme,' sighs Belinda, turning over, snuggling under the bed-clothes, wriggling her legs down to her toes.

'Might do just that,' says Colin. He looks down at his sister and nods. 'Just exactly that.'

There is a little spring in his step. The taxidermist is an amusing ploy. As he goes along the passage he encounters his Aunt Annie. He waves the peacock aloft. 'Rejoice and be glad,' he cries, 'for behold, thine enemy is no more.'

She gives a little shriek, not perhaps immediately understanding what's what, and tittups quickly away in the direction of the kitchen. Colin saunters out of the side door into the yard where the cars are garaged. He tosses the peacock's body into the back seat of the old Daimler which he is no longer permitted to drive, and extracts the keys from the locker where they are kept, and starts the engine. The sun is shining winningly, quite clearly God is up there in his heaven, the lark, if not the peacock's, on the wing, Colin feels happy. Just for the moment, with the promise of the taxidermist, things are hunky-dory. He might have an expensive but nutritious breakfast at the Station Hotel. There is nothing like a kipper after a night's drinking.

As he drives through the country lanes, he sings to himself a little song:

'se vuol ballare, signor contino.'

There is no significance in the words, but Mozart equals things temporarily O.K.

While Colin drove through the milking morning, Belinda, stretched straight again in bed, drifted back to a chequered sleep, in which memories walked, ghosts put on pleasant flesh, and vague desires were audible. The island of her sleep was full of noises; summer-like they gave delight and did not hurt.

In the kitchen Annie threw open windows, sprayed airfreshener from the aerosol, and sniffed in disapproval. There was a snap of moral authority in her rapid step. She went through to the hall and rang Diana in her London flat. She did this daily now. It was important to keep Diana, who was so busy, in touch. She told her Grace was sinking fast.

'Belinda,' she said, 'went for a walk with young Kenneth Leslie yesterday. They walked in the woods to the sun-dial. This though Oswald was here too. Bare-faced behaviour I call it, bare-faced and shameless. I thought you ought to know.'

She had no image of Diana at the other end of the line, merely the conviction of energy and worth.

When she put down the receiver, she went to the front door to collect the post. There was one letter for Colin. She took it, tittuping, to the kitchen where the kettle was ready steaming. It was one of the most satisfying moments of the day.

Colin drove through country that became richer, greener, more luxuriant. Old woods, planted by the first agricultural improvers of the eighteenth century, fringed the road; then gave way to fields of grass where shiny black cattle were already feeding. Later in the day they would go down to the river and stand ankle-deep for hours in the shallows. Then there were fields where the corn was golding. And then on his left, as the Daimler cruised in its billowing way, blank walls, blank roofs, and, in a moment, a sign, pointing down a bare-verged arterial road, that read 'Pottersfield Industrial Estate'. Immediately a child's village of neat little houses succeeded it, subtly varied with the same degree of stylistic difference that Fords parked in front of some houses showed from Datsuns or Marinas before others.

Men and women were emerging from houses, sometimes accompanied by children, and getting into cars to go to school or work. But Colin had swooped by into the old centre of the city, where within a few minutes he had parked the car outside the Station Hotel.

He ate a breakfast that was an exercise in nostalgia, the sort of meal he now had perhaps twice a year. Probably he'd never had it much more often than that—though throughout his second year at Cambridge he had certainly had a cooked breakfast, either poached eggs on toast or bacon and eggs, at the Whim café—but in the past this had seemed the right, the natural sort of meal to have. It was the normal way to live, even if, most of the time, he departed from that norm. Now, ordering porridge, kipper, poached eggs, rolls, toast and marmalade, he had the sense of consciously indulging in fantasy. On the other hand it was very good. The kipper might be as he suspected from a Canadian herring; it was still capable of arousing the reflection that if he ate that every day, he would be a wiser, better and happier man. Healthier too, shouldn't wonder.

He passed on the suggestion to the waiter, but the waiter came from the Philippines or somewhere and failed to grasp his meaning. Colin sighed, and poured another cup of tea; he had cautiously eschewed the coffee.

He lit a cigarette and looked down the large dining-room, empty but for the waiters and a party of eight or nine Japanese gentlemen, who were breakfasting in silence at a table in the bow window which overlooked the lawn where he had several times played croquet. He glanced over at the doorway where there seemed to be some flurry. He saw Mansie Niven apparently disengaging himself from the head waiter. Mansie noticed him and waved. Colin benevolently acknowledged the wave by raising his cigarette, and in a moment, Mansie, Adam's apple bouncing, was with him.

'What a stupid man that head waiter is. He tried to tell me breakfast was finished. I told him who I was and that I wanted beef, cold roast beef; we'll see what he comes up with.'

'I gather,' Colin said, 'you had a triumph last night.'

Mansie, he was aware, was still a little drunk, though in a different fashion from himself. Mansie, with his bloodshot eyes and slurred speech, seemed dislocated drunk; Colin was ethereally disembodied, swimming drunk; a far finer sensation.

'Poor old Martin,' said Mansie, 'I don't hold it against him, tell him that, not now I've won, though you'd think, wouldn't you, that he'd have had more confidence in me, old school and what not. Fact is, Colin, Martin's always been jealous. Jealous of me, jealous of you, doesn't do, jealousy, simply doesn't do. Look at me, I'm incapable of it. I say, tell you what, what about some champagne?'

'Why not?' said Colin. 'I've got to see my taxidermist, but that's my only engagement.'

'Taxidermist, that's a good one, who're you stuffing today?' Mansie laughed uproariously.

'The peacock,' Colin said, 'found its corpse this morning.'

'The peacock,' Mansie said, 'that's bad. It was good seeing Belinda again. Made me realize what fools we've been, getting married to other people. Ought to keep these things in the magic circle.'

'Absolutely, in the family I always say.'

'Tell you what,' said Mansie, 'let's be really silly for once. Let's have pink champagne.'

They'd some difficulty in placing the order, but experience and tenacity triumphed. A magnum was commanded, and, having arrived, was consumed, though they were persuaded to carry it through to the lounge soon after the Japanese gentlemen left the dining-room. One of them returned with his camera and a flash.

'You don't think he's Press, do you?' said Mansie.

'No.'

'It is my constituency, y'know, and this wouldn't look good in the Press. They'd make something of it.'

'What are Belinda's plans?' Mansie asked when they were settled in their armchairs in the lounge.

'Belinda's plans? How should I know? Haven't the foggiest, we're not great planners.'

Mansie crossed his legs, uncrossed them, crossed them again, and waggled his left foot as if trying to throw it off.

'Is she actually divorced?'

'If you ask me it's all one to her, marriage, divorce, that sort of one, doesn't signify much.'

'It's better to make the cut-off, that's what Susie and I decided. She said to me, "Mansie, nothing will inhibit you and I'm off." And she upped and offed. Mind you, I did well enough out of it. I never made your nineteenth-century mistake, Colin, and married for love, I married for money, and look at me now, well-pelfed and a man of property. Good eighteenth-century way of conducting your life.'

See post

'Oh yes,' said Colin, 'always found the eighteenth-century over-rated myself.'

At eleven o'clock the bottle was empty. Mansie said, 'Think I'll toddle up to my room and have a bath and shave. Why not come up, we can get another bottle . . .'

'Got to get to the taxidermist,' Colin said. The idea was coming to have a dominating importance.

'Of course, of course, but tell you what, we'll meet for a drink afterwards, in the bar here, twelvish.'

Colin went through to the lobby and retrieved the peacock from the hall porter.

'I say,' a young man said, 'do you see that, it's surely out of season.'

He spoke to his blonde girl-friend, but Colin courteously answered, 'There is no close season for peacocks. The pea-cock is not a protected species in any way.'

The girl said, 'But you didn't shoot it, did you?'

She had a face of ineffable silliness and a voice to match. Colin for a moment hesitated. 'No,' he said, 'though they make good eating. This one is, or rather was, on the old side. When I lived in the Hindu Kush we used to roast them over braziers.'

'Heavens.' She opened her eyes wide.

'Heaven too.'

'But what are you going to do with it?'

'I am this instant on my way to the taxidermist to have it stuffed.' He gave them a polite inclination of the head and made for the swing doors.

'I told you Scotland was weird,' the young man said to the girl.

Belinda woke at last with the sun streaming in. She still woke cat-like, slowly. Her hangover was mild, leaving her not feeling so much ill as perhaps possessed of sharper per-ceptions. The grass looked greener, the blades more separate. She went downstairs, found the kitchen deserted and had some coffee. Then, with that guilt she had experienced ever since the nurse's arrival, she made her way to Grace's bedroom.

Nurse was there, solidly there, the room her property.

Belinda said, 'Dr Craig hasn't been yet?'

'Never a sight of him.'

'He said he would be sure to look in . . .'

'It's always a comfort to see him. Your aunt peeked in a while back. She saw me here and made off with a mutter. She's not right in the head, I'm thinking.'

'Oh well, she has her eccentricities, lived for a long time by herself you know.'

She was immediately aware that this remark was short of tact; Nurse was a spinster herself. And what was she now herself, come to think of it?

'Why don't you,' Belinda said, 'get some fresh air? It's a lovely morning, I'll stay with Grace.'

'I won't say no, I'll tell you that, I won't say no.'

She gathered her belongings, pushing them with soft red pudgy hands into a black capacious bag.

'You're looking a bit peaky yourself,' she said.

'I'm not sleeping very well.'

'No, that's the way it is at this stage; you'll sleep long enough when it's all behind you. I can tell Colin isn't sleeping either. Is there somebody could maybe drive me to the village, I've some messages I'd like to do.'

'Oh dear me, that's difficult if I'm to stay here—Colin's gone to Perth. You might find Peter, you know, Mr Begg who lives in the lodge, he would do it.'

'He's not very polite, Mr Begg.'

'Oh dear, he can be difficult.'

Nurse stood, clutching the bag to her bosom, waiting for the solution to be given.

'In that case,' said Belinda, 'ring the garage and ask them to send a car. Charge it to us of course, and get them to bring you back also. They're usually quite quick.'

She was glad to be left alone with Grace. The truth was, she shouldn't have agreed to Patrick Craig's suggestion that they get a nurse. It had been the worst sort of mistake, allowing her to slide back into herself. She wondered if she should just tell her to go. But the communion with Grace that her arrival had broken wasn't going to be restored. It was only a matter of days—and then she would anyway, even more urgently, be face to face with what she should do next.

Deathbeds were only interruptions to the business of living. The business too of loving.

Colin, distrusting his ability to park in the narrow streets, took a taxi from the hotel to the taxidermist. He pushed the half-door open, which action tinkled a bell, and stepped down the half-step into the half-light. The old man looked up, over the top of his half-rimmed spectacles, and took a pinch of snuff from the open mull on his work-bench.

'It's some years since I was seeing you,' he said, 'but you're wearing well man, wearing well.'

'*Tempus fugit*,' Colin said, 'I'm glad to find you still in business.'

'I'm not the retiring kind. What would I do now? What's this you've brought me? Oh yon's a bonny bird.'

'The last of the flock.'

'I mind soon after the major bought them, there was a fête held in the gardens and I was admiring them. "I promise you the stuffing of them, Archie," he said to me. It's the first one I've had though.'

'Well,' said Colin, 'I don't think I've come on a corpse before, or I'd have let you have it. Taxidermy seems one of the few living art forms. Some of the birds I know just flew away, into the forests. There was one at least lived there a long time. I suppose the foxes got other ones, I don't really know. You can make a job of this then?'

The old man took the bird from him and laid it on the bench. He ran his hands over it like a surgeon.

'I'm sorry it's the first, the whole flock stuffed would have made a braw sight. Still that's the way the world goes, promises, promises and you're lucky to hae any fulfilled. Lucky indeed. It's a good thing he's died when he did and no' in moult.'

'You can make a tail erect I take it?'

'Oh aye, easy enough, it'll be a pleasure to work on it, a change from hamsters from the council estates; there's a great run on stuffed hamsters these days, the dirty brutes.'

124

'Yes, indeed, not much *sic transit gloria mundi* about them.'

'No' a great deal. I'm sorry to hear the old lady's sinking.'

Colin nodded. He looked round the crowded room. The old stuffed vulture that had terrified him as a child and delighted him as a boy, was still there. The old man interpreted his glance.

'Oh aye, he's still here, is Theophilus, and no, Colin, you canna hae him. I mind fine how you've aye hankered after him, and I mind your wife once near cajoled me into selling him. A young lady with a charm it needed all my wiles and resolution to resist. I hope she's keeping fine.'

'Thank you for asking. I'll let her know you remembered her.'

' "I want it as a surprise," she kept saying to me, "for his birthday. Have it hanging over him when he wakes." Then she was ettling at me to let her borrow it, but I wasn't having that either. "It's no' moved from this shop since my father's time," I tell't her, "and it'll bide here to pick ower my bones," I said. She's a rare girl, that's what I tell't her, "you're a rare lass, Mrs Meldrum," I said, "but yon's a *rara avis*, and that's by way of being rarer." Made her laugh, that did. You tell her I mind that fine and ask her to look in when she's next by.'

'I will indeed. And when do you think you might have it done by?'

'There's the stages, shall we say the end of the month?'

'The end of the month will be fine.'

'And mind now, my regards to Mrs Meldrum.'

Regards to Mrs Meldrum are not quite in the day's programme, but Colin nods, and leaves the shop, eyes blinking in the sunlight. What he has left though is something that seems at once strange and right as he looks across the street and up and down it at the other shops. To maintain his mood, he goes to Rattray's the tobacconist to buy cigarettes and cigars. He puts them on the account. It is still the account there and he supposes somebody pays it. They receive him with the deference they accord to a customer who doesn't even have to say the account but just picks up his purchases and walks out. Grandpa Major used to buy an ounce of Old Gowrie and 25 Hoyo de Montereys every week, except those many weeks during and after the war when he had to take such cigars as were available. When he was in London he had the tobacco sent but not the cigars. Colin didn't know where he had bought his cigars in London; probably simply Fortnum's.

He lights a cigarette which makes him cough, and for a moment he rests, after the coughing, with one hand pressed against a rough-cast stone wall. He looks for the moment less than the man who strolls into Overton's and orders a dozen oysters and an imperial pint of Bollinger; but he is aware of it, and the awareness draws a smile from him. What he needs, rather imperatively, is a drink. Back to the hotel.

Mansie is down in the bar, and is bathed, shaved and scented. He looks better in disarray, dapper is the word for him now; even perhaps natty. He greets Colin in lordly fashion and waves towards his companions who are, Colin is not surprised to observe, the young man and the silly girl he had earlier encountered in the lobby.

'Lost your bird?' says the young man, who is predictably called Robin.

'Why, it's the man with the peacock,' flutes the girl.

Colin acknowledges their presence, but only just.

'Business is concluded for the day,' he says, 'we are now free to pursue pleasure.'

Curiously Colin's words darken nobody's mood, not even his own.

Robin says, 'We're strangers here. I'm actually Scottish myself, but I've lived all my life in the South, I haven't been in Scotland since I was a child. We used to go to the seaside here, it sounds awful to think of. It's Sally's first visit though. We both think it's marvellous.'

'You are lucky to live here,' says the girl.

'Mansie only just lives here,' Colin says. 'He labours in the common weal and must perforce do that in London.'

'People seem to have so much more fun here,' Robin says.

'We stayed for a few days with friends who have a place on Deeside. Out of this world.'

` 'Hilarious,' Sally says.

Colin looks across the room. The barman wears a tartan jacket these days. Their glasses are empty. Colin sweeps them up and takes them over to the bar. He wouldn't have had to do that here once.

'Same again,' says the barman.

'Yes,' says Colin, 'put it on Mr Niven's bill, will you. I dare say Parliamentary expenses can stretch to it.'

Colin waits at the bar and gazes into the mirror. He can see Robin's face reflected. The wrong way round, it is twenty years ago. When the barman puts the gins before them, he drinks one very quickly and says, 'a re-fill here', before turning and carrying the others to the table. Then he goes back for the replenished glass. Turning and turning, between bar and table, it is like being a hamster in its wheel. He doesn't tell the barman this, but looks him straight in the eye instead.

'Are you an actress?' he says to Sally.

'You are clever,' she says, 'how did you guess?'

'It's just a gift,' Colin says.

'What do you do yourself?' she says. 'I'm sure it's something very interesting.'

'Nothing.'

'That is interesting,' the boy Robin says, 'it's my ambition too.'

'I should think you could achieve it,' Colin says, 'Mansie here does a more damaging nothing, he's a legislator.'

'I never was any good at maths myself,' says Sally. She opens her very blue eyes very wide, as if she has made a joke and the boy Robin, seeing this, laughs.

Mansie speaks in an avuncular manner, this new gin is making him suddenly soppy-drunk, tears may flow at any moment, 'You young people have your lives before you.' As observation, it is not exactly A1. Colin can tell that the boy has his best years behind him; his promise flowered between fourteen and sixteen, while Sally is now in her fullest bloom.

Still, politicians must be permitted their rhetoric and fantasies. No doubt Mansie is going to tell them what they must do with these lives they have before them. But he is interrupted. Another party has entered the bar and they are Gavin and Fiona, Kenneth Leslie, Gerald Morgan and his servant Kwame. Surely Kwame is not going to be allowed to drink with the others?

They stop suddenly. It is a small bar and there is no possibility of avoiding each other. Colin leans back. Mansie springs to his feet. This is a bit ambitious. He lurches against a chair, but manages to steady himself.

'I saw the Daimler,' Fiona says. 'Is Belinda with you?'

'No,' says Colin, 'I came by my little self.'

'Pushing your luck, Colin,' says Gavin. 'Bloody risky, I'd say. You'd better not drive back. One of us'll drive you.'

'Oh,' Colin says, 'is this a posse?'

He observes Kenneth smile, but all the others ignore the remark. Meanwhile, the boy Robin has come a step forward.

'Kenneth,' he says, 'this is terrific. Sally, this is Kenneth, he was in my house at school.'

'Oh yes,' she says, 'super.'

'We must have a drink,' Robin says.

'There's clearly,' Morgan says, 'been a hell of a lot too much of that already. Niven, we had an appointment. Kwame,' he speaks rapidly in some African tongue, and the lean Negro comes forward, takes Mansie by the elbow and leads him out of the bar. It is done with an economy and assurance that casts a chill on the party. Who next? It is like the four o'clock knock on the door. Mansie makes no protest whatsoever.

'It is his weakness, Gerald,' Fiona puts her hand on Morgan's sleeve, 'I told you it was.'

'Weakness,' Morgan snaps, 'I'll flay him.'

He turns on his heel and advances to the bar. He speaks in low, rapid tones. The barman nods his head, mechanical doll-style. Morgan stalks out towards the hotel lobby.

'What a pity,' Colin quotes, 'that so great a man should have such bad manners.'

Fiona is near tears. She bites her rubious lip.

'You don't understand,' she says, 'how can you both be so childish? You don't understand how important it is. The whole thing could be blown just like that, by one incautious word.'

'If it's important,' says Colin, 'count me out. You see,' he says to Sally, 'how lucky we are to live here. Peter Pan also ran—when it comes to fantasy, wha's like us? Bloody few, an' they're a' deid. Well, I don't know about anyone else, but I need a refreshener. Gavin, you old booby, you look as though a rather large Scotch would improve your morning. Don't worry, we'll charge it to Mansie.'

'I don't think I should,' Gavin says.

'Hilarious,' says Colin.

Gavin has got himself into a situation he can't discern; all he can do if he hopes to keep on the rails, is succumb to whatever will is turned in his direction. That's generally Fiona's, and here of course Fiona is fortified by Morgan. The poor red-faced puffing fellow hasn't a hope. He's like the wretched steers Robert Cohn was sorry for at Pamplona. At least Julie had been subtler in her attempts at control. It is after all very embarrassing for a chap to have to say he doesn't think he should have a drink—especially when he hasn't the acknowledged excuse of a drink problem to offer. Perhaps a wife problem?

'Oh come on,' Colin says, 'just a quick one?'

But Gavin can't be moved. Young Kenneth, however, is made of different mettle.

'I'd very much like some gin,' he says.

'Good for you,' Colin says, and they both look Fiona in the face. When she drops her eyes, theirs meet, shining. Colin turns to the bar. The barman has vanished.

'There seem to be obstacles to the having of the fun,' Colin says.

'Fun,' cries Fiona, 'what fun is there? Oh Colin, for God's sake, stop.'

'Could it be,' Colin says, looking at Robin, at Sally, at Kenneth, 'that a move is called for? Things seem less than hunky-dory here. Apart from which—there's always something to be said for evacuating cities—it's not every city that can be designated open and so safe from bombs. A move to the country perhaps—what do you say?—I have the car outside.'

Glances are exchanged as Fiona is left standing like a pedestrian at a traffic island, caught between changes of traffic lights. The young are willing, even eager. They will accept whatever they don't know. And Colin says, 'It looks anyway as though service has been discontinued here. Is this Morgan's long arm interfering even with the sacred dispensation of liquor?'

Robin, though ignorant of Morgan, laughs, for it is obviously a joke. Fiona must be desperate. She looks at Gavin.

'Here, I say,' says Gavin, 'don't think this is a frightfully good idea. Don't think you should drive, Colin, old thing. Take a breather, eh?'

'What are you going to do, Gavin, call the police?'

'It would serve you right,' Fiona says, 'if we did.'

'Ah,' says Colin, 'but you won't.'

Annie waylaid Belinda, the first time in days.

She met her with a disapproving sniff.

'It's not decent,' she said. 'It's not decent.'

She danced before Belinda, blocking the doorway, the way out, like the awakened conscience. Belinda looked over her shoulder to where the sun struck the far side of the yard where two cats basked.

'It's ungodly,' Annie said, 'I've had to let your mother know. I felt it my duty. It's time you came up, I said to her. To darken Grace's last hours with revelry and viciousness! What time I would like to know did Dr Craig leave last night?'

'Patrick Craig, what's that to do with you, Aunt Annie?'

'It's my business whether this house is turned into a den of vice. Seven years I've made it my home, out of decency and care for others and now you come with your . . .'

She chattered, face empurpled, words dancing around each other in a mad reel, 'your lewd practices,' she finished, 'your lewd practices.'

And there was nothing Belinda could say in reply, for it was of course true, if you looked at it from a certain standpoint. What happens in the mind is as real as in the flesh, and not only did she wait for Patrick Craig to speak last night—and would have answered yes, with a weary nod—but ... a breeze from the courtyard blows her hair over her eyes, bringing with it too the scent of flowers, and memories of the south, of broken columns, tumbling roses and a wine-dark sea. The corruption of the flesh betrays the spirit, but you can read that more than one way.

'A house of the dying.'

Soon to be, of course, a house of the dead. Honour the dead, lament the dead, mourn their passing, celebrate their lives. When Byron and Trelawny had watched Shelley's body burn on the Lerici shore, and seen the brains bubble, they got riotous drunk in the homeward carriage.

'There's no excuse for it, that I can see. It's just not decent. I'm disappointed in Colin, but then he's always been weak. You've ever been able to lead him as you wish.'

'Colin? He's obstinate as a pig.'

Inevitably the Daimler drew up before the Graham Arms, the journey having been accomplished with no incident, though passengers less blithe might have experienced alarm.

'You had no need for fear,' Colin said, 'I only crash when sober. Motto, therefore, never be sober.'

'Is there much danger of that?' said Kenneth.

'None, for nowadays I only drive when drunk. *Ergo*, I have eliminated risk. You are about to see Scottish life in its less rosy aspects, though at least there are no vanishing bar-men here, and credit is still good. Putatively good.'

They settled themselves at the bar, which was in fact empty except for a drunken labourer having a day off in the corner. Mr Smith's greeting to Colin was tolerant rather than effusive; but tolerance was all Colin sought, even in his present mood. They arranged themselves on stools, Colin and Kenneth flanking Robin and Sally, Colin getting his back to the side wall, between the small window, which was above bar level, and the open fire. It was not lit and a cat slept in the grate. Colin started by holding court. He told them of an expedition to Paris years ago when he had found himself, under the influence of many Pernods, explaining the principles of Existentialism to a shabby old Frenchman.

'He surprised me by having a goodish grip of them, which is something no lecturer ever asks for from his audience, so I pitched it a bit strong, getting more and more abstruse, and was just thinking I was on the point of baffling him, when the waiter came up and said, *"Téléphone, Monsieur Sartre, c'est une jeune fille qui parle . . ."* '

'I've never drunk Pernod,' said Sally.

'No time like the present for remedying that. Do you have any Pernod, Mr Smith? . . . alas . . . alas, *sic transit* . . .'

He told them of an expedition to the Alps where there had been no snow and they had ended up in Zermatt, drinking the worst white wine in the world—'Joyce used to like it, which I've always held accounts for Winnegan's Fake'—and 'my friend Giles petulantly kicked a hole in a huge plate glass window and was immediately, but immediately, surrounded by hordes of Switzers all extending their hands, palms uppermost . . . it's a very comfortable country, Switzerland, despite the white wine, all you've got to do is pay. You can pay for anything, do what damage you like, as long as you've got wads of Swiss francs to shuffle out. Mind you, it's a mysterious country too. Would you believe that in the Gare des Eaux-Vives, which is a little suburban *gare* in Genf, the *specialités de la maison* are Nasi-Goreng and Malayan Chicken Curry? Rum.'

He ordered more drinks—'on that faithful slate, please, Mr Smith. That's where Scotland differs from Switzerreich, there are things you can't buy here.'

'Such as love?' suggested Kenneth.

'Love, my dear, is for sale everywhere.'

He told them of a May Ball in Cambridge which a sometime Financial Secretary to the Treasury had attended in
drag—'a King's man, of course. You're not at King's, are you?'
he asked Robin.

He told them of many meetings, comic, bizarre, ridiculous,
of trips to Paris, trips to Rome, trips to Naples, trips to
Provence, of how London had declined from a leathery
imperial city to a sleazy clip-joint, he told them of encounters
with gamblers (of a great coup at Monte Carlo), with pimps
and politicians, with actresses and gigolos, with Negro boxers
and with a man in a little bar in Rome who had proved pain-
fully to be the judo expert he, Colin, was claiming to be. He
told them, he told them, he lost them and in the end didn't
so much run down as find a vacancy. He said nothing of death
in all this, nor of the corrupting worm. All was jollity, nothing
funnier than the odd disaster. 'You mustn't take anything too
seriously, baby,' he said. 'My friend Jack once shot a policeman in Athens and lived to smile at the recollection.'

Kenneth said, 'That chap, Morgan, who came in with my
my brother and sister-in-law, the one in the safari jacket;
don't have anything to do with him. He's a nasty.'

Sally shifted on the bar-stool and crossed her white cot-
toned legs. She said, 'Look, there's a dartboard. Do you play
darts?'

She and Kenneth slipped from the bar-stools.

'Robin,' she said, 'is no good. Keep the score Robin will
you.'

'Keep it yourself. I'm having an . . .'

Sally put the tip of her pink tongue between pink lips as,
with deft concentration, she threw her dart. Her neat buttocks pressed themselves against the white seat of her pants,
as, on tiptoe, she threw a double twenty.

'Who is this Morgan anyway?' she said. 'He looked rather
dishy, I must say.'

Kenneth threw more casually.

'He's a thug,' he said, 'from Rhodesia or some such place.
I wouldn't have anything to do with him, if I were you. I think
my sister-in-law's a fool.'

'Ooh,' she said and threw a triple twenty.

'Hey, not so fast, you're rather good.'

'There's no point playing games if you're not rather good.'

Kenneth eyed her. 'Quite,' he said, 'you rather bear that out.'

'You must have known a lot of interesting people,' Robin said to Colin.

Colin looked at the two faces reflected in the mirror. 'You would like to meet interesting people,' he said.

'Well, they're better than bores, aren't they?'

'They are bores . . .'

Their hair grew in the same way, smooth out the lines and it was the same face. Colin could see that, though Robin couldn't. It was easier to read the past than the future.

Why are you living up here now?

Are you afraid of what you will come to?

Colin raised his empty glass and looked at Robin through it; so also the sand ran out of the hourglass.

'Where I made one', he said, 'turn down an empty glass.' He did so. 'Mr Smith, could you oblige . . .'

Grace woke and opened her eyes. They were clear, though looking a long way off. Belinda felt a gentle pressure on her hand. She responded. Grace wet her lips with her tongue and the lips moved. Belinda couldn't make out what she said.

'Would you like some tea?' she said herself.

Maybe the head moved. Belinda anyway made tea, Lapsang, weak but fragrant. She held a cup to Grace's lips and damped them. A little, a very little, was swallowed. Grace rested back, relaxing. Belinda took her hand again and squeezed. They stayed like that a bit.

'There'll be more money than you maybe expect,' the words came in a soft inanimate whisper, stifled as velvet stifles. 'More money. Property, I bought and sold in the boom. I knew . . . you and Alastair, no good about it. Brought you up like that to be no good about money . . . so . . . response . . .'

'Don't talk, darling, I understand.'

It is terrible that Grace should be thinking about money now, even if, in doing so, she is thinking of others; but the dying should be cared for, not occupy and distress their last moments caring for the morally weak who will survive them. The room is darkening. Nurse has not returned from the village. Perhaps she has decamped.

Response . . . you and Alastair, you and Colin surely . . . you, Colin and dead Alastair.

The clamorous caw of rooks crosses the paling sky towards the pine wood.

Colin and Robin walk by the river, in owl-light. The grass is damp with dew. The trees are not quite black.

'Colour of verdigris? The word sounds right though I don't know just what the colour is . . .'

Beside them, the river courses, deep, swelling, pregnant, towards a destination that ought to be unknown. Sally and Kenneth have disappeared; at some point in the evening, as the Graham Arms began to fill with labourers, small farmers, tradespeople, Sally and Kenneth had simply not been there.

'Not, I fancy, a philosophical problem. But rivers are, or rather pose one. You know Heraclitus. It's odd to think, Robin, are you thinking it, that you will walk by this river in, what? twenty years' time, with a younger self, and I did so, what? twenty years ago. Does it frighten you? It ought not to frighten you. When I look at you, I see that it couldn't have been otherwise, and when you look at me, in this distorting hall of mirrors, you should at least feel some reassurance, even if only of the Abbé Siéyès type. You remember Siéyès? What did you do in the Revolution, Abbé? *J'ai vécu.*'

'Trouble is, it's terribly like Sally. She just strings along with me, you know. I can never rely on her for a moment.'

'In that case you are promised a beautiful liberation. You don't really believe you are what you are, do you? Let me prove it to you. In your Cambridge rooms you have a set of Proust, with a gap between *Sodome et Gomorrhe* and *Le*

Temps Retrouvé, in the Chatto and Windus edition, Scott-Moncrieff translation.'

'What a coincidence,' says Robin. 'It's strange to see Kenneth disappear with her.'

'Well, don't wheek about it. Girls come and go, life goes on . . .'

Grace died sometime that night. The nurse woke Belinda and said, 'Come, I think she's going.'

Belinda put on slippers and dressing-gown and hurried to Grace's room. She couldn't immediately detect any difference in the still figure. She said to the nurse, 'You'd better get my aunt. Yes, do, it's only fair that she should be here too.'

Half an hour later, Annie said, 'Well, that's it.'

She drew the sheet over Grace's face.

'That's it,' she repeated, 'she's been a long time about it.'

Belinda shuddered. She went to the window and stepped behind the curtain and opened the bottom of the window and looked out. The woodwork felt cool and damp, but crumbly. There was a mist in the air, clinging to the branches of the trees, obscuring the line of the bushes, hiding the distance. No sound at all, except an interrupted gentle dripping. Then there was silence and a little breeze, keen on Belinda's face. She opened her lips to it. It died away and the rain began. She stood watching it for what seemed like a long time, as from a slow, gentle, dripping, moss-soft start it swelled into a downpour that rebounded violently from the teak benches on the lawn. Belinda put her hand out, cupped to receive the rain. She carried rainwater to her mouth and sipped. She turned and walked out of the room, past Grace who had become or was becoming (for did some sort of consciousness survive the hour death was pronounced?) simply the body.

She opened the front door of the house, letting the wet morning air enter in a mighty rush. Still in her slippers, but throwing a raincoat round her shoulders, she stepped out into the thudding rain and squelched across the lawn, cutting the corner of the curving drive. She walked straight, with her head back, eyes grounded stars, along the drive towards the gates. From the gates, the valley stretched wet and wild-wooded away in the greying morning. She perched on a broken gate-post as the light grew. Presently a car turned off the road towards her. It braked sharply. Patrick Craig thrust his head out of the window.

'Belinda,' he said, 'what the hell?'

She slid off the gate-post and came towards him.

'I was out on a call,' he said, 'I only got the message when I got home.'

'It doesn't matter: She's gone though.'

'I guessed that when I saw you here. You'd better get in, for Christ's sake. It'll be you next. You don't want to catch pneumonia, do you? I'm sorry I wasn't there though.'

'It doesn't matter, I wasn't really waiting for you, and no, I wasn't trying to catch pneumonia. Not my style. I just wanted to get very wet, to drink up the rain. I don't know why.'

'It's the sort of time, sort of occasion when it's natural, to do things without having any idea why. A symptom of shock. Do you want something for it?'

'No, why should I. She didn't suffer at the end. Just slipped away, between one breath and another which didn't come.'

In the hall they found Annie replacing the telephone receiver. Her eyes sparkled.

'I got Diana,' she said. 'She'll catch the first shuttle. She wants us to send a car to Edinburgh for her. That'll be a weight off my shoulders. Dr Craig, I'm not surprised you were too late. Since you're here you could maybe take a look at my bunion.'

IV

Diana filled the house. Not with her luggage, she had only
brought what she usually took for a week-end, but windows
had to be opened to accommodate her. Curtains and furniture
and glass looked worn and shabby; Diana had chrome where-
ever she went. The telephone caught the animation, the
drawing-room on the first floor breathed again, radios crackled
with news bulletins and pop music served as background to
her *maquillage*. Andrew had come with her—'who wouldn't
choose to see Diana ascendant, ducky?'—and Kevin in un-
zipped cardigan—'*blouson jaune*,' said Andrew—flexed
aggressive muscles.

'It's absurd at this moment of time, the idea of burial,'
Diana said, 'I've called the crematorium.'

'You don't understand,' Belinda said, 'the arrangements
have been made.'

'Arrangements are always better re-arranged. I can't stand
sloppy sentiment.'

Kevin sniggered, 'I've never met anyone like your Ma for
being on the ball.'

'Grace hated cremation.'

'Oh stuff. I've no patience . . .'

'Nor authority,' said Colin, entering the room. '*Les jeux
sont faits*.' He turned the radio off.

'Do you mind,' said Kevin.

'Yes, as a matter of fact, yes.'

'Tut-tut,' said Andrew.

Belinda was counting hours. It was absurd that they should
not bury Grace as and where she had wished. She couldn't
understand her mother's attitude; that was her first reaction,
but it wasn't of course true. Dust to dust and the giving of the
body to the laily worm, it was an acknowledgement of what?
Tradition, heritage, relationships; for Diana better by far the
service flat, the quick anonymous affair to the intricate and

testing relationship with its shifting dependencies; not that she herself ... and she looked across at Andrew, who, greying, curly-headed still, and dapper-poovy, was enjoying the contest which he only too well understood. What was the sexual act without love but a cry and rejection, the assertion of the ego that would powerfully choose to consign the fine-spun web of feeling to the flames? Make every day a clean new hygienic start and where were you? If community was dead and relationships could not be sustained, well, it might be better to admit it and confront the devil of the vacant stairway than to try to cheat him.

Colin looked long and callous at his mother.

'There's one thing you seem to have forgotten. It's got nothing to do with you, Mummy. This isn't your trashy magazine. You've no power to make decisions or over-ride those that have been made. No power but what your threshing about gives you, and that's only what others are prepared to accord ...'

And he left the room.

'Belinda,' Diana said, 'you may not have noticed it, but your brother has gone quite nuts. He ought to see an alienist. I expect it's only drink, but when I think of your father I can't be quite sure.'

Kevin laughed.

Diana froze him.

'God,' she said, 'I'd forgotten how absolutely bloody and provincial it is here. Everybody cracked. It's like living in a hothouse at Kew. Only it's cold and damp. Where's your sister Fiona?'

'Fiona, she'll be over.'

'She might have had the manners to put in an appearance. You're looking terrible yourself. Crow's feet. Honestly, why you allow yourself to go to seed, I don't know. When I think of what I was doing at your age, it makes me sick. It makes me positively sick to think how bloody wet my children are. Oh yes, you too, Andrew. Do you know, Kevin, four of them and I've got two grandchildren that's all. Two, pumped out of them. What a generation.'

What would please Diana would be for the house to catch fire.

Belinda sits on a stool before the empty grate and looks at the arabesques that trace themselves in the Turkey carpet. With the pale fingers of her right hand she plays with a kitten, scratching the underside of its jaw, losing the tips of her fingers in the black softness of its fur.

'You know I hated Grace when you were young, I don't mind admitting it. The way she worked to steal you children's affection; that was before I realized what that sort of affection was, blood-sucking, parasitical . . .'

Colin went ahead with arrangements for the funeral all the same. He saw the local Episcopalian minister. He said to Belinda, 'Have you a black dress?'

'No, of course not . . .'

'I'd like you to get one. I want it done properly, with decorum. I've fixed with Macrae's the caterers to lay something on here.'

Belinda caught the mood. 'I think I would have to go to Edinburgh.'

'Well, go tomorrow, it's fixed for Friday. There will be a service at St Kentigern's. She'll be buried in the churchyard, and then back here.'

'Why do you think our mother is taking this attitude?'

Colin looked out of the window and dug his hands in his pockets. The corners of his mouth turned down. 'Look at the life she leads.'

'You think that simply explains it?'

'Nobody could really think it's a good way to live. So she spits venom, Andrew's the same. I don't claim much for my own way of living, you know that well, and I don't even claim something wet like "it doesn't harm anyone", but it's not indecent.'

'Fiona's worried, you know, she telephoned and said so. She actually telephoned just to say so.'

'Well she would be. The trouble with our little sister is that she's not worried about herself.'

'What do you mean?'

'Oh nothing, I never mean anything . . .'

But the evasion was too late. Colin despised Fiona because she worried from the wrong side of the fence. All her emotions, her moral attitudes, her enthusiasms, were ignorant. His own were different; he was after all tired of being Colin, even if he wasn't going to do anything about it; Fiona had never considered the question of being Fiona.

'All right,' she said, 'I'll get a black dress. I'll drive to Edinburgh tomorrow and get one. You're quite right, but this is very head of the household stuff.'

'Well, I am the head of the family.'

Belinda telephoned Kenneth and asked him if he would like to come to Edinburgh with her.

'Why not,' he said.

Andrew cornered her in the kitchen.

'What's this I hear,' he said, 'ducky, that you're going back to Oswald?'

'Of course I'm not going back to Oswald.'

'You could do worse. I know he's of a ghastliness, but he has money . . . or has Grace left you all hers?'

'I don't know, we'll find out when the will's read. Not that I suppose the will will be read, as they do in detective novels, but I suppose the lawyers'll tell us what's what. You're looking very sleek.'

'Oh well I have to, the Bank expects it, and of course with my temperament . . .'

She looks coolly at Andrew who has always seemed so at ease with his temperament. She cannot imagine Andrew with five o'clock dawn horrors.

'I don't know if I've told you'—it has always been Andrew's way of conveying information which may be greeted with mockery—'I don't know if I told you, I'm going into politics. I've been lucky, I'm likely to inherit a safe seat . . .'

'Good God, you . . .'

'I've made myself useful in lots of little ways.'

141

'What about . . .' she searches for a way to put it '. . . your temperament?'

'Oh that, no problem there, I'm always circumspect, and again,' he runs his tongue round his lips like a cream-fed cat, 'I'm lucky there too, you know. My tastes have never run to rough trade. The boys I fancy are neat-bummed business boys, the kind who've as much to lose as I have, it makes things ever so comfortable.'

'When you say business boys,' she can't help asking.

'I mean just what I say, not renters, no no nothing like that, neat little chaps who work in estate agencies and banks and building societies, because that's where Mummy has directed them, in their smart little suits and just daring perhaps to put a half-inch on their heels. And they suit me. The trouble with you and Colin, ducky, is you're Romantics. In the last quarter of the twentieth ghastly century, you still have a picture of yourselves that was formed a long long time ago. I bet you anything, when you were sitting by Grace, you kept on looking at that photograph of Uncle Alastair, the original poor little lost boy. All that dreary J. M. Barrie stuff. We've all got to settle for something a lot less than dreams these days. Do you have any idea of our position in the world, personally, nationally, politically?'

As Andrew speaks Belinda finds her hands, trying to make coffee, shake so that the metal top of the coffee pot tinkles against the metal base and she has to put it down, press her palms against her buttocks and bite her lip.

'Would you like some coffee?' she says.

'Oh yes.'

'God, I'm so tired.'

She would like to sit down but she tries again and this time is able to screw the pot together.

'All the big thoughts,' Andrew says, 'have been thought, and they look pretty shabby and empty to me. I know you and Colin have always had a low opinion of me, you've always laughed at me. Grace had no time for me. It's a long time since I've been worried by it. You see, I know something of what the world's like. I'm the nearest thing we have to a realist in the family, and I play only winners. We are crummy little islanders in a crummy little island, and there are too many of us, so some of us have to support the rest. And if we've any sense we'll go on doing it, because the alternative's a damned sight worse, ducky. That's the starting-point and, within the scenario, you can live comfortably enough, if . . . what precisely are you going to do now?'

Too many people are going to be asking the question.

'Grace was your last excuse, ducky.'

Oswald telephoned Belinda. 'I'm sorry,' he said, 'I won't be able to see you again, and sorry you've turned down the offer.'

'I thought,' she said, 'it wasn't coming off anyway. Fiona told me Mansie's speech had mucked things up, that he'd blown it. Morgan was furious, she said.'

'Gerald over-reacted. It's his weakness, I'm glad to have been here to see it, it's caused me to revise my ideas of his desirability as a working partner.'

'You mean, you're breaking it off,' she said. 'For your sake, Oswald, I'm glad, he's a nasty, you know.'

She could read infinite patience in the sigh that the wires brought her.

'No, you misunderstand me, it's merely a matter of re-assessing the role Gerald will play in the organization . . .'

'I don't understand. You mean you're going on, Mansie's boob wasn't quite so boobish . . .'

'It mucked things up quite sufficiently. Only I don't give up good ideas as easily as Gerald does. No, the press coverage will be bad. That's why I can't see you again. I'm off to London to pick up the pieces. I'll get something on television. That'll clear things up.'

'How on earth?'

'Newspapers are in politics and that's bad, but the telly's show business. If we can make it show business the boob doesn't matter. In show business it's fine.'

'That was more or less what Oswald said. Do you understand it?' Belinda now asked Andrew, to change the subject.

'Of course, he's got a certain acumen. In show business anything goes. Get something on TV—he's quite right—and it becomes morally neutral. Politics on television are operating in the same world as "Coronation Street", "This Is Your Life" and so on, ducky. There's no difference between Robin Day and David Coleman, or Ena Sharples and Maggie Thatcher (much though I revere *la serenissima*); they're all characters in the great ongoing soap opera, don't you see.'

'Not really—it sounds rather far-fetched to me.'

(Silly clever-little-bugger stuff, Colin was to call it) . . .

Late summer night lapped like lake water on the shore about them, as, in candle-light, they assembled, in answer to a gong, in the L-shaped dining-room for supper. Colin has insisted to Belinda supper be served there and had himself telephoned Fiona to ask her and Gavin to come across.

'What on earth do we eat? There's not much in the house, it's not as if we've been going in much for cooking.'

'That's all right,' he said, 'I've arranged for Mrs Thomson to send us a ham from the village, and I've bought salad and cheese and fruit. A cold meal will be perfectly suitable.'

'And any meal will be rather ghastly,' said Belinda, 'considering circumstances and company.'

'Martin and Jill will come too. I telephoned them also.'

She looked at Colin. 'What are you trying to do? Is there something behind this?'

Colin shook his head. 'If you mean,' he said, 'am I planning anything, the answer is, certainly not. We've got to get through the next few days, and it's better we set out to do it in a certain style. That's at least suitable. I'm not going any further than that. I appreciate of course,' he sipped his whisky-and-soda and flickered his eye out of the window in the L of the room, 'that style may be beyond us. Let's at least give it a chance.'

Style is indeed likely to be beyond them, if by style Colin means what Belinda takes him to mean. Yet there is style in the room this evening, only . . . it's a long way from Edwardian. Actually Diana is in a sense the only truly Edwardian figure there. Not in age of course—but because she alone, Belinda can't help granting, goes at life with a certain attack that you could call panache. See her introduce Kevin to Fiona, knowing exactly how Fiona feels, and savouring the knowledge.

'Kevin,' she says, drawing back her lips from her teeth (which are very fine, professionally fine) 'this is Gavin. Fiona married him. He's a landowner, his grandfather built bridges and railways. He filled a canal with Irish navvies.'

'Maybe my great-grandad was one of them?'

Gavin doesn't quite know how to take this visitation of his ancestors' sins.

Fiona says, 'That's the sort of way things happened. Heavens if we were all to be held responsible for . . .'

Martin and Jill arrive. Martin is losing his ruddiness; in less than a month he has simply diminished. His eyes avoid Diana's. Belinda is aware they are seeking hers, but she busies herself at the table where the drinks are set out. Jill looks as though she has come under protest. She is carrying a beaded handbag, and she swings it to and fro, knocks it against the sides of chairs, lets the beads sparkle in the light, so that it is less a handbag than a shield.

Eventually they all have drinks. Belinda has now no excuse to remain at the side table. She picks up her own glass, finding the Martini which Colin insisted on shaking, icy and cloudy against her fingers. She sips.

'This drink's far too strong,' says Fiona, 'it's ridiculously strong, is there any fruit juice?'

'Over here,' says Belinda, who finds the Martini just right, and very invigorating.

'Kenneth seemed to have vanished. I wasn't able to give him the invitation.'

'I didn't know . . .'

'Oh yes.'

They stand together, making no doubt a beautiful picture, the two elegant sisters framed in the rose-fringed window—

where is the *Tatler* photographer who should snap them? Kenneth hovers immaterially between them. Belinda knows that Fiona can't quite dare to say, 'it would be better if you stopped running after him, you will upset him, give him all sorts of false ideas.'

Instead however, now armed with pineapple juice, she says, 'Have you met Sally?'

'Sally?'

'Yes, she's a friend of a friend of Kenneth's, called Robin. We came across them in the Station Hotel. She's very lively, he less so. There was talk that they might all go fishing, in one of the hill lochs. I hope they have. You've no idea how irritating I've found it all this summer, having Kenneth simply drifting about, really just mooning, and always with this ghastly air of being superior, though how anyone so aimless can claim that I for one can't tell. Of course he's terribly young for his age, you've no idea how immature, sometimes, I tell him, you'd think you'd just left Prep School, not Eton. Of course they couldn't make anything of him there. His housemaster simply despaired. The boy's got some ability and talent, he said to me, but it's so latent you'd think it was stillborn. So I hope he takes up with this Sally. From what I've seen she's brisk and lively and go-ahead. But what she could see in him, I mean, it's simply wishful thinking to think that any girl with go about her could see anything in him, at least as he is now.'

While Fiona has been delivering herself of this, Belinda has also been aware of Kevin hovering in their vicinity, obviously eager to talk to them. And she glances across the room and sees that Diana has indeed managed to collar Martin, that she has manoeuvred her upholstered body round in such a way that Martin has been driven to rest his shoulders on the grained-marble chimney-piece, while his head is pushed back on his neck, so far that she can see reflected in the glass a balding spot.

Kevin now pushes forward and says, 'Fucking good Martini this. Your brother has at least that going for him.'

'You'd like another,' Belinda says.

'Aye, wouldn't say no.'

She is irritated by the affectation, but reaches across and seizes the shaker and pours some into his glass and into hers.

'You know, it's strange to me this set-up. I'd no notion Di had this sort of set-up. Christ it's like something out of one of those Ealing Comedy films I saw in the Stockport Odeon as a boy . . .'

'What exactly do you do?' says Fiona in her social, distancing voice.

For a moment Kevin looks at her through candid eyes, and Belinda, though she doesn't respond herself, is aware that he is exercising a certain magnetic force. It flashes across her mind that he might reply in ghastly precision of detail, but he only says, 'I'm a photographer, a fashion photographer mostly.'

'I see' says Fiona, 'you work on Mummy's magazine then?' She gives a swift smile, because this information can ease everything.

'You could put it like that,' Kevin says, still looking Fiona steadily in the face, steady gaze directed at a mouth that is less sure at the edges than it's wont to be. 'I wouldn't mind photographing you, I wouldn't mind doing you at all, I could make something bloody good of you.'

Fiona blushes.

Belinda can hear music where there is no music, she listens to the twang of instruments that move the feet. They are in a dance, the steps are there, pre-ordered, choice is dead. Certainly the measures are intricate and the patterns ever-changing, hard to trace as arabesques in the Turkey carpet.

The ham has been consumed, wine circulates, the mood ought to be mellow.

Diana, however, though assiduously tended by Annie— 'You'll take a tiny spot more, won't you?'—is not in mellow mood. She sits at the end of the table, Colin opposite, and flanked by Kevin and Martin. She speaks across Kevin to Fiona, who is crumbling bread, but who has eaten with keen appetite.

'What's this I hear, Fiona, about you making a fool of yourself, over that old bugger, Gerald Morgan?'

'Language, Mother,' says Colin, but no one pays any attention, 'and accuracy,' he adds.

Fiona looks up. She is in awe of her mother, but she knows what is right.

'I don't know what you mean, a fool of myself. I don't make that sort of fool of myself, but I happen to believe in Gerald. I didn't know that you knew him, or anything about him, Mummy . . .'

'I've known Gerald Morgan since I was a girl. Your father knew him well too, and he was a bag of wind from the beginning. Didn't Grace ever tell you about him? Do you know that when he was in the Army, his commanding officer had to post a guard over his tent in case one of the men cut his throat in the night. That's the sort of brute he is.'

'I've met him,' Kevin said, 'he's a filthy fascist. A racist.'

'Oh racism,' says Martin, 'we're all a bit bored with that sort of talk. That's not an issue here, though I'd agree Morgan strikes me as a dirty bit.of work.'

'What do you mean it's not an issue here, it's the issue of the time we live in, isn't it Di?'

'I mean it's not an issue here, because it's a phoney issue here.'

'Christ, what sort of world do you think you're living in?'

'Morgan ponces around with that African servant—that could make it an issue,' Colin said. It is wicked of Colin to say this, because it is pure mischief-making.

'Don't be silly, Colin, Kwame's devoted to Gerald.'

'Do you know, darling,' says Andrew—and how innocent Andrew looks—'Do you know, I was talking to an old general in the Club the other day, a sweet old thing, who'd just come back from a nostalgic visit to India, where he'd served as a—what's that dishy thing, Martin?—yes, a subaltern in the days of the Raj, the dear old Raj. And do you know what he said to me?' Andrew's voice becomes gruff and his neck disappears into his shoulders—'They lie down in the dust and touch your knees and they say, "Sahib, when will you come back, sahib, when will you come back?" So ducky I know just what you mean, and I'm sure, yes utterly positive, that Kwame's devoted to Gerald.'

Diana flashes a smile at Andrew. 'It's extraordinary,' she says, in that tone that freezes editorial conferences, 'that the only one of my children who knows a damned thing about anything should be a little nance like you, Andrew.'

'The meek, ducky, shall inherit the earth.'

'Comes of living in the real world,' says Kevin. 'You can't be expected to see how things really are, if you live in the outback. I learned that when I left Stockport. Mind you, Morgan takes a marvellous picture too. All the corruption of imperialist-capitalism in a single snap . . .'

'Oh God, Mother, what have you caught this time?' says Colin, with the bored, indulgent tone of one who turns to say good-bye to La Rochefoucauld. 'Haven't we heard all this before . . . ?'

'You may have heard it before, sure, but that doesn't mean you've heard it often enough.'

There is no doubt that Kevin has spunk. He's a bit above the cut of Diana's usual young men. His ideas aren't of course formed by reflection—whose are?—but they are fierily expressed. Belinda feels a sudden apprehension for her mother—it could be she's bitten off more than . . . but when she glances across at her, the serenely-powdered face destroys the argument. Diana doesn't care a hang for Kevin. There is though the question of pride; in all affairs of the heart it is the feeling most easily wounded. We may love others, ah yes, but self-love is deeper and more persistent. Belinda begins to gather the plates.

'I take it,' she says, 'that everyone would like raspberries.' She starts to dish them out.

'It's easy enough,' she hears Gavin say, 'to laugh at the Empire. I get a bit fed up hearing people sneer at it, to tell the truth. After all you can't get away from it, it was the Empire that made us great. Haven't been much, have we, since we lost it?'

The two portraits on the wall nod in approval. One is

Grandpa Major, dressed in the uniform of the local Terri-torials; he, in a more functional but less impressive uniform, did his bit for Anglo-Egyptian relations while serving in the Canal Zone in the twenties. The other is his grandfather, General Sir Angus Meldrum, born 1828, who served forty years in India and may have been the first through the breach at the relief of Lucknow in the Mutiny. The VC he won on that occasion glints on his chest. There is no portrait of the intervening generation, great-grandfather—Belinda can't even put a name to him, but, while not exactly dis-graceful, he had lived a number of years on the Continent (mostly in Naples or on the Sorrentine peninsula—a number of not very skilful landscapes testify to his residence there)—married late and briefly and died of something or other. Belinda ought to be able to put a name to him, because she has sought out his grave in the Protestant cemetery in Rome.

'Yeah, well,' says Kevin, 'it didn't do much for the working-classes, did it, and I'm Lancashire Irish working-class.'

('How banal,' Colin murmurs.)

'So you can't expect me to exactly enthuse over it. You won't find many bloody Indians or Africans to do so either. And what's the point, it's finished.'

'You are absolutely right there, ducky,' says Andrew.

'Yes, but . . .' says Fiona.

'But nothing, baby.'

'That's not really the point of what Gerald says, he's not interested in restoring the Empire, he's a realist and he says that however good a thing was, when it's gone, it's gone for good, for good or ill. That's not the point. What is, is quite different. It's the way we carry on, pretending everything's for the best in the best of all possible worlds and that people are basically good, I mean Voltaire exploded all that nonsense, didn't he?'

'Well, I dunno, by and large in my experience people are not bad. Take my old grandma, Di's met her, she's a great old girl, isn't she, yet she was on the game for thirty years. There's moralists would condemn her fast enough, your fucking Gerald Morgans, but she never had a bleeding chance and she was determined to give me one . . . I don't call that bad.'

'She sounds super,' says Fiona, and Belinda is surprised Diana has nothing to say about the gallant old trouper.

'But there you are you see,' Fiona says, 'she wanted you to get on. That's in tune actually with Gerald's way of thinking. It shows an acceptance of hierarchy. You know *Measure for Measure*, "but when degree . . .", I can't remember just how it goes . . .'

'For Chrissake . . . that's not the point,' Kevin flashes his heavy gold watch as he throws up his suede-clad arms in protest, 'I don't set myself up as being better than my granny. I don't accept his bloody ranks, there's no fucking rungs on the ladder I'm on . . .'

'You can't quite call it a ladder then,' says Fiona, sweetly scoring a point.

'So you've got there at last, it ain't no fucking ladder,' and with these words, he looks back again at Diana, who sums it up.

'The trouble with you, Fiona, is you still think wool has to come from sheep'.

'Bull's-eye.'

And in the whole evening there is no word of Grace.

'So what exactly do you know happened?'

'Well, I came downstairs . . .'

They are sitting, Kenneth and Belinda, in a cellar restaurant in the New Town of Edinburgh. It is principally a hamburger restaurant, Kenneth has chosen it on the recommendation of some friends. 'Authentically New York,' one of them said, but it isn't quite that. Still, the food is fine, the helpings substantial, Belinda's salt-beef sandwich excellent in fact; and the room is decorated, even adorned, with blown-up photographs of Hollywood greats. They are sitting under Bogey, just in position to get his cigarette smoke in the eye.

'And there were Fiona and Kevin—that's his name isn't it?—tangled on the sofa. Fiona's skirt was rucked right up.

Sounds unpleasant, but I could actually see his hand. Well, naturally,' Kenneth blushes, 'I didn't for a moment know what to do. My first reaction was to stop him, tell him to stop at any rate, because Fiona, well, you know Fiona . . . she's, I'd have thought, the last person, the last girl anyway . . . but, this was the extraordinary thing, she wasn't protesting at all. In fact . . . look I can't go on, it makes me sound so horrible, as if I was some kind of voyeur, just standing there and taking it all in. It wasn't like that at all, I don't suppose I was there more than half a minute, but I could see Fiona was co-operating. I thought of coughing, because for all I knew Gavin might come in . . .'

'Not a chance of course, but you couldn't know that. The whole point was that Gavin passed out.'

'He's doing that rather often these days.' Kenneth reaches out his hand for the bottle of Bernkasteler, as he says this, and pours two glasses.

'And Kevin volunteered to drive them home,' she says.

'Was Fiona plastered too? I've never known her be.'

'No, she wasn't. Fiona doesn't much like drink, you know. She just made it clear that she didn't care for driving a drunk Gavin. Something about how he'd once tried to grab the wheel.'

Kevin had been very quick to volunteer. Even then, Belinda had no doubt of what he hoped for. She wondered if Fiona knew. Surely she did? You couldn't not know something like that. She looked across the table at Kenneth, with Bogey looking quizzically, commandingly, above him, with his eyes creased against the smoke. Kevin, who wasn't big, had slung Gavin across his shoulder.

'Fireman's lift, only way to deal with drunks.'

'So I slipped away,' Kenneth says. 'Wasn't after all anything to do with me. What I didn't like was my reaction to what I was seeing.'

'That's natural.'

'What time did Kevin get back, do you know?'

'No, I don't . . . of course I don't.'

'I was wondering, obviously if . . .'

152

For a few minutes they eat in silence. There is a thumping drum rhythm to the music that is loudly, constantly played. They could be anywhere; it is hard to remember that just outside, up the stairs, sun shines bright on clear, cold Georgian streets; though of course the one immediately outside has been defaced by nineteenth- and twentieth-century shop fronts. Only now are they attempting to insist that restoration be carried out, that any new developments are in keeping with the original style; with the result that they look dead. What they have is not purity and chastity; not at all; simply they are aseptic.

'Did you catch any fish yesterday?' Belinda says.

'Fish?'

'You went fishing, didn't you?'

'We set out to. Somehow we got sidetracked. Sally liked the idea better than . . . and Robin's quite hopeless. Have you met them?'

'No.'

'Thought you might have. Colin had them back for a drink, or Robin at least. I've known him for years. He was in my house at Eton. Before that we were at Prep School together. He's a couple of years older, but we played in the Eleven together. Robin's O.K., even if he's not going anywhere. Perhaps because. I don't much care for chaps who obviously are.'

'And Sally?'

'Sally's a slut. Quite fun.'

There is absolutely nothing significant in this, except that it's impossible, if you read things right, for anything that is said to be without significance.

Belinda changes the subject. 'What shall we do after lunch? I never thought I'd find a dress so quickly. Miracles never . . . so we've the afternoon.'

'You haven't said if you like my haircut?'

'I thought you mightn't like me to comment, but, yes, actually I do.'

'I thought I'd better . . . for the funeral.'

'That was nice of you. I told you about Diana, didn't I? Wanting cremation . . .'

'I went to a cremation once. It was the nastiest thing.'

The waiter brings them some ice cream and coffee. Belinda says, 'thank you', and then, to Kenneth, 'Do you like looking at paintings?'

'Depends.'

'Somebody told me that in the National Gallery, they have two new Turners from the Rosebery collection, I'd rather like to . . .'

'Why not . . . Turner's O.K.'

They turn a corner in an upper room in the gallery and, at once, straight before them, but a long way ahead, is a shaft of light emerging from a golden smoke. A city grows into being as they approach it. The twisting snake is the river, the Tiber. On the other bank the Customs Houses of Papal Rome, when the city was its own port and boats came up the river, stand out clear and new, as seen from the Aventino. Away to the left gleams the great Michelangelo dome. The whole painting catches and, for just that instant that is eternity, stabilizes moving light.

Belinda stands there before it, feeling the silence of the gallery first cling to her and then fall away, as the gallery itself is dissipated in this swimming light. Her belly aches. A nerve in her left eye twitches. She senses that her lips are moving gently, that the corners are alive, and in the middle they press together. She is aware of this, but it is all swallowed up in the shimmering reality that is before her. Kenneth is beside her; after a minute, he drops back and sits on a bench in the middle of the room, and, in a little, she feels that his gaze has shifted, that it is now directed at her.

She turns round. On the other wall is a darker Rome. The Forum, Palatine and Colosseum, caught from the Capitol in evening light. Troops of religious walk dotted in irregular arrowhead formation across the darkling plain; white-clad figures hold the Cross aloft. Heads are bowed. Immediately in the forefront of the picture, where the rock begins to tumble down to the valley, goatherds recline, half-watching their straying charges, half-watching each other. Hands turn contemplative straws and grasses that their small teeth (doubtless blackened and diseased) nibble. In the distance, golden with last rays of the sun, rear the Alban hills.

There is of course nothing to say. The goatherds know this, though they could put no words to their knowledge; in them essence equals existence with no gap. Not that this is what Turner is setting out to say; he has painted a picture. What it is and what comes out of it is a rearrangement of sensibility. But essence equals existence? It is a long time since Belinda has experienced that, even for moments. She can't explain anything of this to Kenneth, and, she wonders, of course she wonders, if he, in any way, feels the same.

In any way.

'It's super,' he says. 'They're both super.'

She points her finger towards the right of Trajan's Column, which itself just gets in on the picture's extreme left.

'At one time,' she says, 'I lived just here, behind it and out of sight, in the Suburra. A low life area in imperial days. Not so very *higlif* now, not at all in fact, but very agreeable. I loved it in fact. Piazza dei Zingari—Gypsy Square— and I did my shopping in the Via dei Serpenti—Snake Street.'

'Are you going back there?'

'Yes,' she says, 'I think I am.'

They go downstairs, cool marble living stairs. They pause at the great Titian which represents, in wonderful ordered symmetry, 'The Three Ages of Man'.

'You see,' says Belinda, 'for Titian, there is only one age that is really alive, to all human possibilities.'

It may be a mistake to say this, instead of just thinking it.

'I like the babies too,' says Kenneth.

'Do you know about Titian? He lived to be ninety-nine and it took the Plague to kill him then.'

They skirt the gallery walls quickly. Kenneth stops a moment before a Greuze of a girl with a dead sparrow. She has a perfect face and perfect hair and pools of grey eyes. *Passer meae puellae*, he doesn't say.

They look at the Revd Walker skating on Duddingston Loch, in his black suit and top hat and perfect poise of Presbyterian certainty.

'Christ,' says Kenneth.

'There's no doubt,' says Belinda, 'he knew he was one of the redeemed.'

'Look at his linen. Blood of the Lamb washes whiter, even than Persil.'

They come on an absurd Victorian painting, the meeting of Oberon and Titania. Kenneth begins to laugh.

'Gosh, it's super. Did you ever see such a ponce?'

'Do you think the model for Oberon was a girl . . . or just a fevered imagination?'

'Where's Bottom, he ought to be there?'

'You're quite right, you can't possibly have Oberon and Titania without Bottom too, just to keep you . . .'

But sentences like this are better not finished. There is of course something in it, wherever the state means more than the object.

'Would you say Kevin?' he asks.

'Ah,' she says, and wonders, yet again, how her mother has taken it.

'You know that girl Sally?' Kenneth says.

'Yes,' she answers cautiously.

Kenneth doesn't immediately reply.

'What about her?' she says.

'Nothing really . . . she's a bit of a slut. I thought at first she fancied your brother. Colin, of course, not Andrew.'

'Well, tough on any girl who fancied either, if you ask me.'

But that's only what he thought at first?

They walk out and along the street, on the gardens side, where tourists sit on many benches, taking the sun. They cross the gardens under the shadow of the Castle Rock, and over the railway and turn left towards the Grassmarket. They are not walking to any purpose but the pleasure of strolling together, and yet there may be something beyond that that directs their steps. The Grassmarket they find in shadow.

Their lunch and the gallery have taken more of the afternoon than they had allowed for.

'I've never been here before,' Kenneth says.

'It's changed since I used to come here, not that I came often. There was a time when it was slumming to come here. You'd be bold to enter one of these pubs. I remember coming with Colin once, he nearly got smashed.'

'You can still see why.' Kenneth indicates a group of men who are congregated, some of them standing, the others sitting, round a doorway with two or three bottles, more or less empty, on the ground between them.

'There's a couple of lodging houses for them.'

Belinda is aware of a slight nervousness as she passes by, but all she gets is the sort of look cattle give; it occurs to her that these are past the reaction she feared. They go up the hill and over a rise into the High Street and then down the Canongate, dark and glooming towards Holyrood.

'But it's nothing like I remember,' she says.

'How come? It looks impressive, it's remarkable.'

'These prissy antique shops, souvenir shops and the deadness. It used to be thronging, a pretty sad sort of life but undoubtedly a sort of life. You might be frightened here, but . . . it had something of the vitality of Rome or Naples. If this is what conservation means, we can do without . . . I mean it's appalling . . .'

'Don't look so miserable.'

'I can't help it. This used to be the finest street in Europe, with wonderful contrasts and a line, what a line . . .'

'Well the line's still here . . .'

'Only goes to show it wasn't the line . . . oh well.'

She takes Kenneth's hand and presses it. She feels the separate bones, barely covered by flesh, rub against each other. But there is a response, which the hand of a skeleton could not give. The response is real. Kenneth disengages and puts an arm round her shoulders. It lies lightly there.

'I'd no idea,' he says, 'you felt like this about things.'

'Oh things, you feel about things. In Scotland of course I always feel guilty, one way . . .'

He waits for her to go on.

'There's a pub there,' she says, 'let's go and have a drink.'

There is nothing much to recommend the pub either. The walls have tartan covering and the tables sad formica tops. The gantry is modern and the three or four people already drinking have the air of mournful tourists, except for a big man in braces sitting studying the evening's dog card.

'What'll you drink?'

Belinda looks around. 'Beer, I think it'll have to be beer.'

'I'll bring it over.'

Belinda composes herself, which, for many reasons, is necessary. Things are out of hand. Grace is dead, she has to keep hold of that, it provides at the very least an explanation of the way she feels. An excuse for her then, but Fiona wouldn't have been sufficiently affected by the death to merit one, and yet her behaviour . . . Of course, the workings of the flesh . . . she supposed Gavin's flesh hadn't worked for a long time, while carnality played no part in Fiona's devotion to Morgan, which was an expression of sublimated lust, so that when Kevin with his brash 'I want' appeared before her, it was easy to see how it had worked out. Whereas she had had enough of brashness. Still, after all Fiona's pious moralities, and her own acceptance of them as being essentially Fiona, well they would both have to eat their words, silly, ghastly expression.

The trouble with this city was it couldn't decide whether it was a museum or a place to live in, a capital or a shopping centre; it didn't know its own essence.

She is glad to see Kenneth return with drinks.

'I took you at your word, got us pints of heavy.'

'So I see. I don't know if I can. I haven't drunk beer like this since I was at St Andrews.'

'I didn't know you were there.'

'Yes, it was all right, I like it. Very relaxed. Goodness, it's strong.'

'Why do you always feel guilty in Scotland?'

'Why do you ask? Don't you?'

'I don't often think about Scotland.'

'But you are Scots?'

'Oh yes.'

'Doesn't that answer your question?'

'Does it?'

'I don't know. I can't stand almost anything that manifests itself as Scots. Tartan and this beer, and Billy Connolly and Morningside and hard men or football supporters . . .'

'Well, who can . . . I mean that's not the whole of Scotland . . .'

'No, but . . . it's terrible to be ashamed of your family.'

Night has fallen as they leave the pub, though it is not yet dark. The air gives a velvet intimacy to them. Kenneth's arm is more firmly upon her shoulder. They have said nothing directly about themselves in the pub, but they have come closer. And the new weight of the arm on the shoulder testifies to this.

'What shall we do now?' Kenneth says. 'It's too early to go home.'

'I don't want to go home. I don't want that at all.'

Grace's body rests in the first-floor bedroom behind drawn blinds and drawn curtains.

They have come up the hill again. On their left looms the dark jagged mass that is the High Kirk of St Giles. Belinda looks long at it; sound of sermons thud through the windows. Here morality is enthroned and wears a horsehair wig on its head, starched petticoats on the lower portions of the body. Belinda's fingers tremble. She feels a little sick but the beer alone cannot be fairly blamed.

She turns her face to Kenneth and asks him.

It hasn't worked. They both know that. Hotel bedrooms always contain threats of failure, for inevitably they take something away from the act, unless perhaps they are set by the sea, existing for the purposes of lovers, who can all in those surroundings play at being honey mooners.

Not so here, where a train entering the three o'clock city rumbles below them, and blows a whistle, doubtless late.

Perhaps it is the barren imagination of the hour conjures up the whistle. Belinda presses her face against the pillow. She knows Kenneth is awake too, now in the other bed.

It wasn't just the discovery of twin beds, which shouldn't anyway have been a surprise. That had certainly introduced an element at once furtive and impersonal. There had been a moment of embarrassment while they decided which to use. But it hadn't been that. They simply hadn't come together, however tenderly they tried, however they wanted it. It hadn't taken fire.

Belinda stretches out her legs, long model legs, and bites her lip and waits for the morning.

Perhaps she has thought about it too much, both have thought about it too long; there was certainly no question of an assault on the city . . . whereas Fiona and Kevin, theirs must have been just like that . . . She feels ashamed of herself, and for Kenneth, who, in the morning, long-lipped, long-lidded, brooding . . . perhaps it will not be necessary to have breakfast.

At four she is weeping; at five she gets up to have a bath.

Fog surrounds them, thick haar come up from the Forth, whence even in her bath Belinda hears the steady drone of horns. Fog hangs over the awakening city; from the breakfast room of the hotel even the monument to Sir Walter Scott, huge and only a few yards away, is hidden in a shroud of fog. Fog's fingers are felt stretching into the room, the waitress's eyes are touched with it; it comes between them. When Kenneth speaks there is fog in his voice, and when they go outside they find it cold, damp and gnawing too.

Towards Queensferry and the Bridge across the firth, fog is thicker still. Lights shine dull orange and yellow, traffic is at foggy crawl, roadside trees and tall trees in suburban gardens are all swathed. For once there is no wind to stir it.

They cross the invisible river. Held up by a line of traffic, they are for a moment in limbo suspended over moaning boats, at last creep forward to the refuge of the northern shore. But, before they do so, Belinda has a momentary image, image in the mind's eye, nowhere else, of the pall of fog stretched over the coffined valley of central Scotland, fog from Forth to Clyde, seeping even in its inertia along the sour valley, curling its fingers round classical façades, rubbing on the window-panes of the high courts and tenements, breathing through the corridors of the administration, yellowing, blackening, souring the stonework. It extends across the country, enveloping towns whose names thud like a litany in her ignorant ears—Bo'ness, Grangemouth, Bathgate, Motherwell, Airdrie, Coatbridge, many more—until at last, coiling and then uncoiling itself, it descends, a deadening blanket, on the docks and yards of the west.

Of what goes on within the fog she has an ignorance that cannot even imagine.

Kenneth's profile is sharp against the grey outside. A tooth is pulling back his lower lip.

So they drive back in a silence made acute by failure, the numbed effect of having done badly that which ought not to have been done at all.

Fiona was on the lawn when they returned.

'What on earth,' she said, 'I was thinking we would have to send out search parties.'

But she was not really interested, Belinda could tell that. She accepted her explanation, that the car had needed something done to it, for an electrical fault it had developed, without enquiry. Belinda even wondered, as she gave the explanation, whether it was worth giving. Who cared?

'Mother telephoned,' Fiona said, 'I didn't say anything, I said I had no idea, but I gave her to understand Kenneth had come back. She sounded ramping and I didn't see why I should help. Do you know, it's extraordinary, Belinda, it's as if I'm seeing Mummy for the first time, I mean I've always stood so much in awe of her before, at least since I was eleven or twelve and she stopped being nice to me.'

'I suppose I'd better get back.'

'Kenneth seems to have vanished, Really, that boy's manners. He might at least have said thank you.'

'For what it's worth.'

'Oh you've done a lot for Kenneth this summer, Heaven knows, he's been intolerable but he'd have been even worse if . . .'

Belinda began to feel like a social worker.

'Would you like some coffee? It can't have been much fun driving in the fog. It hasn't been bad here and it cleared about half-an-hour ago, but I heard about it on the radio.

'Coffee? Why not?'

Fiona began to speak about the dinner the other evening. She thought Martin had been looking absolutely miserable. 'And Jill looks at the end of her tether.' She didn't think that marriage was for much longer, though she couldn't see quite how it would break up. Of course Belinda would know more about that than she would. Poor Aunt Annie had aged terribly. She didn't know whether she would really be able to look after herself much longer, even if she got the house back in Broughty Ferry, and she gathered there were difficulties there. She would have her here, but that wasn't in fact so easy. Apart from the question of room, and that could be solved, wasn't actually a problem, she wasn't sure Annie would like being a complete dependent. 'Not when she's always been so independent herself.' There were other obstacles too. Gavin didn't really like her, and it was of course his house after all. Had Belinda made any plans? She assumed Grace would have left her money. It was obvious. Belinda had always been the favourite. Belinda and Colin. Colin would get the house. So Belinda must get some money. She herself after all was well enough provided for.

No shadow crossed her face as she said this; all was innocence and sun and contentment.

Had Belinda thought of where she would live? She wasn't thinking of getting married again, was she? It depended of course on whether she got a job. What sort of job? Had she thought that she and Annie might live together? Fiona knew it sounded a bit abrupt and could see that there might be difficulties of temperament.

'Difficulties of temperament? You might as well ask Andrew to have Annie in his flat.'

'Oh Andrew. If you ask me, he's heading for disaster. It's become so blatant.'

'I think people like Andrew are much safer if they're blatant. Anyway, who cares nowadays?'

The phrase sounded foreign to Belinda even as she spoke it. There were, after all, reasons to care. Sexual manners wasn't simply a phrase to be understood in a neutral anthropological sense.

'Well, I do for one,' Fiona spoke sturdily, 'it gives me the creeps. It's disgusting, I know the media try to give the impression that nobody cares about that sort of thing now, but it's not true. Decent people find it as disgusting as they always have and it's time they stood up and said so and were counted. I was speaking to Mansie about it, he quite agreed.'

'Oh Mansie, he's a fine one to talk.'

'Anyway, I wish Andrew would leave Kenneth alone. That's one of the reasons I was so glad to see you take him up, terribly kind of you I thought it, and then delighted when he seemed interested in Sally, but then I discover that that Robin, who's a pretty awful little shit, is another of them, one of Andrew's set I mean. It's quite disgusting.'

Fiona's face became quite pink as she delivered herself of all this. Belinda sipped her coffee. She felt drained. It didn't come as any surprise what Fiona said, and she wasn't sure it was so very accurate either. It didn't alter facts, the way circumstances were said to alter cases. Not at all; she had set her heart on what wasn't for one reason or another there to be won.

'How's Gavin?' she said.

'Gavin had better pull himself together, the old fool.'

There wasn't much battle though in Fiona's voice. Gavin had served his turn, provided her with what she needed. Still, he must learn not to make a fool of himself in public. It might be useful on occasion—its use had been clear the other night

—but if it became a habit, it would reflect on Fiona, and reflect badly; that wasn't to be thought of. Belinda looked at her little sister with something of admiration; she was indeed looking almost beautiful rather than pretty, the closest she'd come for years to the absolute, stunning beauty she had occasionally promised, and it was evident that Gavin was going to have it tough.

Belinda was tempted to ask Fiona what she thought of their mother's latest, but she looked again at her blooming sister; she was—it would be—transparent. Kevin promised enough unhappiness if Fiona's heart was touched. Probably not though; it came to Belinda suddenly, Fiona was their mother's daughter. Struck by the thought, she for the first time saw Diana as definitely old, an object of pity.

'Here comes the old booby,' said Fiona, and Belinda looked up to see Gavin advance towards them, puffing, red-faced; was there a certain cuckold's hesitation in his stride?

'Look here,' he said, without preamble of greeting, 'it's rather awful, something pretty frightful's happened. I've just had the police on the phone.'

'The police?'

Both girls spoke, it was the inevitable response, what can't help being said, in just that tone, 'The police?'

'Yes, they've had a complaint.'

'Come on, Gavin.'

Possibly impatience was the sharpest spur to adultery?

'Don't take all day about it.'

'It's just that I'm afraid it's going to be a nasty shock to you.'

Gavin swallowed two or three times. Had enough of his classical education stuck to give him a stab of memory of how the Persians used to treat the bringer of bad news?

'It's Kwame, Gerald's man. He's gone to them with complaints. They're going to charge Gerald with assault.'

Belinda kept her eyes momentarily on the ground. The figure in this carpet wasn't so difficult to work out, but she had, for a moment, to struggle against a desire to laugh.

'That's absurd,' Fiona said, 'Kwame's devoted to Gerald.'

'I don't know about that, he's lodged this complaint. Made a statement in fact.'

'Ridiculous.'

'You can't always take things at face value,' Gavin said. He pondered this great thought. 'I mean, they're not always what they seem. It's like marriages. You think everything's fine, between two chums, and then, bang, you discover they can't stand each other, or the husband's been banging the maids or the wife having it off with his best man or the gardener. You just can't tell what people think of each other.'

Pigeons cooed in the tall trees as Gavin said this, and Belinda thought of Andrew's story, possibly invented, of the ex-Indian Army Colonel, and then of how perception so often works inversely to involvement. So Gavin could see that Kwame's relations with Gerald Morgan might not be what they appeared; and Fiona wouldn't.

'What did the police want you for?'

'They just wanted my advice. It's a sensitive case, Gerald's a figure of some standing and a friend of ours. The superintendent knew it might embarrass us. Civil of him.'

'But what are we to do? They'll surely never believe what Kwame has to say. His word against Gerald's, it's ridiculous.'

Fiona didn't actually say, 'a nigger, just down from the trees', but there was no need to. The meaning was clear and indeed, thinking of Kwame's dignity, Belinda thought that nonsense like that was at least clouded by not being spoken. She felt a stab of contempt for her sister; then pity again. It was horrible when stone facings were stripped off.

'You don't understand,' Gavin said, 'it's not just Kwame's word, well it is, but he's got allies. You see, it was Mansie escorted him to the police.'

'Mansie, that doesn't make sense.'

'Kwame wouldn't have dared to go otherwise, he'd never have expected anyone to take him seriously. His word against Gerald's, as you say.'

'But Mansie, it doesn't make sense. Mansie, after all, 's one of us.'

But it did of course. It made sense every way. Mansie

loved the dramatic. Gerald Morgan had humiliated him. Mansie had always had a schoolboy weakness for revenge, the penknife stuck in the fleshy part of the leg, the note dropped accidentally to tell the tale, the innocent wide-eyed revelation of confidences; oh yes, it was Mansie all right.

Gavin still shifted from foot to foot. He put up his right hand and bit a nail. He still hadn't told all.

'Think I might push off and have a drink. Anyone? Belinda, what about you? Sun's over the yard-arm.'

'Gavin,' said Belinda, 'what kind of assault?'

He swallowed.

'Both kinds,' he said, the words emerging like spittle, 'both kinds. Fellow says Gerald used to beat him with a cane, and then bugger him. That's what he says. The police believe him, no doubt about it. It's a nasty business.'

Fiona had leapt to her feet and was running to the house. Her corn-yellow skirt swung vulnerably behind her. She bumped into Kenneth emerging.

'For Christ's sake, keep out of my way, you bloody little poof.'

'Think I'll get that drink. Spot of whisky, Belinda?'

'Yes, I'd like one too. Yes, thank you, please.'

'Poor girl's upset, it's a nasty business. Don't like this sort of thing at all.'

'What's happened?' said Kenneth approaching, 'Fiona . . .'

' 's had a shock,' said Belinda. 'That's all. Don't worry about it. Nothing to do with you, I'll tell you about it though.'

The county and country turned out in force to bury Grace. They came in Bentleys, Jaguars, Rovers, Citroens and Peugeots, Minis and Cortinas, some by bicycle, villagers on foot, one even—old Lady Grizel Borthwick—in a gig. Cars were parked double along the village street; Colin had asked for police to control traffic. Throng moved, heads lowered (so showing in some cases any advancing onlooker the polished crown of top-hats) morning-coated, black-suited, black-dressed, veiled, through air that was soft with recent rain, past gutters glistening sandy-yellow, to the little elmed and yew-treed churchyard, where the rector waited at the church porch to greet them: a short fat man, known always to the family as Wain 45, on account of a newspaper heading many years before 'Wain 45 pleads guilty' (in fact only to some minor offence—not having a wireless licence perhaps). Belinda took his proffered hand with warmth; he was a link to an active Grace—she had been ready to correct misassertions in his sermons. Still, she had only allowed them to laugh at him up to a point; where malice began, she had shut them up. Andrew's mockery had made the point come quick.

He wasn't fat as she had remembered. Looking at him she saw a wasted face. Wain 45 was a dying man too. She remembered Patrick Craig had said he was in hospital; he was explaining why the rector hadn't been calling. He feared cancer.

'I'm glad to be able to do this,' he said to Belinda. 'I wouldn't have liked to have had to hand it over to a deputy.'

'I'm very glad too, I hope it's not going to be too much of a strain.'

'No,' he said, 'it won't be that.'

She passed into the church. Morning Matins, Colin pumping the organ, 'We Praise Thee, O Lord, We acknowledge Thee to be the Lord, All the earth doth worship Thee, the Father everlasting . . .' Summer Evensong, a languorous *Magnificat*. All canticles leading to the *Nunc Dimittis*. Behind her on the West window a trio of martyrs in sub-Pre-Raphaelite colours, St Sebastian, St Agnes and the church's own patron, Kentigern; the choice, evidence of the aestheticism of the builder, a Victorian laird and son of a Glasgow ironmaster. So, a church built by the proceeds of the Industrial Revolution in Ruskinian antithesis to its development.

Grace, with no time for theology, had loved this church; she never went in London.

'I was brought up to look down on the Piskies, the way Annie still does. But St Kentigern's seemed right to me from the moment we bought the old Manse.'

It was a matter of sensibility being in tune; Belinda could feel it too. Live here again properly not waiting for a death, and, yes, she would arrange the altar flowers.

There was a silence. The organ's Bach died away. She was aware of movement. They were bringing the coffin up the aisle. She wasn't sure why it had been arranged like this. Wasn't it more normal to have the coffin waiting there, covered with wreaths, or even straddled on planks across the grave? Colin had insisted they do it this way. And yes, it made it clear emphatically why they were there.

He now came and stood beside her, the coffin rested on a table before the altar.

He was very pale and there was only the faintest whiff of whisky; dressing-room whisky, she supposed.

They prayed. They chanted the psalm for the day. It was something Grace always said, Wain 45 told her later: ' "When you come to bury me, I want the psalm for the day and the collect for the day." You can see why, I think it was a beautiful notion.'

They sang *Abide with Me*—'it isn't my favourite hymn, I admit it's mawkish and sentimental, but it's my favourite funeral hymn, and anyway, I always associate it with the King's death. It was sung in every church in the country that Sunday.' 'Oh well, royalty, my dear,' Belinda had said.

'Earth's joys grow dim, its glories pass away . . .'

Truer than they knew, when was it last possible to use the word 'glory' of any earthly activity, who sought it now? Sporting gladiators, perhaps. She glanced at Colin in profile, singing the next line sternly. Then . . .

'I need Thy presence every passing hour
What but Thy grace can foil the tempter's power . . .'

The tempter's power, the only way to get rid of temptation is to yield to it, it would be nice really to be tempted . . . by anything. She looked at Andrew beyond Colin, not a wish he had ever expressed surely, foiling the tempter's power not exactly in his style . . .

'Where is death's sting? Where, grave, thy victory? . . .'
Where, where indeed?

168

'Heaven's morning breaks and earth's vain shadows flee...'

Up to a point, Lord Copper, up to a ... point. Shadows less than vain darken what's to come.

Then there was movement, eight of them moving, to raise the coffin on their shoulders and carry it to the grave. Colin, Andrew, Martin, being the grandsons; Gavin and Kenneth; Peter Begg from the lodge, who had been Grace's gardener and handyman since Belinda remembered; Patrick Craig, looking the most woebegone of all; and old General Crawford, who had been in Grandpa Major's regiment and still walked erect at eighty, his chest bearing the medals of Alamein, Sicily and the Bulge.

They followed the coffin out of the church to strains of Handel. Grave lay in a corner of the churchyard, under the trees. The river ran under the wall. Grandpa Major's name clear, free from moss, on the stone. Twenty years nearly since his funeral. She'd had a day off school. Dust to dust, she saw Colin's hand crumble the earth before scattering it on the coffin. A moment of silence, the sky held between sun and rain, the air completely still.

A sort of shrugging of shoulders into coats as people turned away, with greetings in low voices.

That was it.

Macrae's the caterers did them well. Colin had decided that he and Diana should greet guests, so Belinda was free from the first to circulate. Colin was putting on a good show.

Now people were relaxing, gossip and exchange of information about families taking over from the silence of respect and mourning. No doubt as it should be.

Margot Rutherford said, 'You'd better get away for a bit, but you'll come back I hope. We need folk like you here, Belinda, question of standards.'

'Maybe,' she said, meaning 'No.'

'You'll have heard of Mansie's effort? D'you know, I'm proud of the loon. That poor bloody nigger.'

Mansie was clearly in high fettle. He wore a glossy, billowing black silk cravat. His coat was cut with an elegance that deserved a better figure. He said to Belinda, 'I'm sorry for

Fiona; I know it must be a blow for her, but there it is. Shouldn't monkey with fellows like that, anyone could see that Morgan was a bad lot, whatever merits his ideas might have.'

'Yes,' said Belinda, 'I gather you used his ideas, his and Oswald's, to save your bacon.'

'My dear,' he laid a paw on her arm, 'ideas are common property. Ideas are the whores of politics. It wasn't anyhow as original as they thought it was. That's the trouble with people who're trying to get in from the fringe. They always think they're saying something new, when really we've been mulling over the same thing for long enough. I'm not saying Oswald hasn't something useful to contribute, but he needs to learn a little humility. Humility, that's the thing. You tell Fiona that. D'you know, I can't help being proud of what I've done there. I wouldn't mind the Kwame case being my political epitaph, not that I'm ready for an epitaph, not by a long chalk.'

'No, Mansie, I don't suppose you are.'

'It's sad about Grace, but I suppose it was for the best. What are your plans? Remember when you come to the decision-making, I'd like a part in them.'

'Oh Mansie.'

She turned away.

She can hear her mother's voice, peacocking remorselessly above the rest. It is an imperial purple voice. She observes Kevin and his eyes moving over the company like one casing the joint, but they come to rest on Fiona, who, in a black suit that strangely doesn't become her, is shifting from foot to foot in boredom. Fiona looks as if she would like to break something, it is not a look Belinda has seen before; things aren't quite so simple for her as they were a few days back.

Kevin, in his light grey suit, too sharply cut, presses his way through the crowd towards Fiona and takes her by the elbow and urges her to the door and out of the room. She doesn't protest. Her skirt doesn't sit right across her bottom.

Belinda looks out of the window. The rain has come on earnestly now.

A tall, grey-haired, stooping man, whom, after a moment, she recognizes as Alastair Moffat, some sort of cousin and Grace's lawyer, approaches her.

'It's been a long time, Belinda,' he says. 'I'm not sure if you even remember who I am.'

She reassures him. He exists for her.

'I was sorry to hear about your marriage,' he says.

She gives a little shrug.

'There's too much of it, I'm afraid,' he says. 'We didn't have it in the family a generation back, my generation I suppose. I hear Colin's is going the same way. He was in to see me, I expect you know that, or I shouldn't have said it, though I find, do you know, I'm getting terribly garrulous. Mary says it's the male menopause but I tell her she flatters me, I passed through that stage years ago.'

She gives a brief flicker of a smile.

'Anyway,' he says, 'this is all informal, but I thought I'd take the chance. It's a simple will. Grace has left most of it to you. The house to Colin, not really hers to leave, small sums to Diana and Fiona. A trust set up, this is the difficult part, to provide an income to Colin for life, when it reverts to the estate, if he has no children, follow that? I'm afraid Grace was worried about Colin. She didn't like the way he seems to be heading, though I must say he's put on a good show today. Impressive.'

She looks at Colin, now standing by the fireplace and bowing over a little old lady she doesn't recognize. She has seen his attitude before, it is quite out-of-date. Ronald Colman perhaps, what a fraud.

'Oh yes,' she says, 'a good show.'

'So you're the ultimate beneficiary. I can't say exactly how much, but I can tell you this, you'll be a rich woman.'

'Rich,' she said, 'I don't understand. Grace wasn't rich.'

'Grace was richer than she thought. She got round to thinking for a few years that she wasn't. It was the inflation. Old people can't handle the concept of inflation. In fact it made her richer. There were a lot of good investments, even one or two your grandfather made. And she bought and sold

171

property in the boom. We did pretty well for her. Oh yes, you'll be rich, and some of it'll keep on growing. Leave it to us.'

He was more confident, competent than she'd have thought. Always imagined family lawyers a bit sleepy.

'It doesn't sound quite right,' she said. 'What about the others? Fiona and Andrew and Annie.'

He gave a smile. She was surprised by its sardonic satisfaction.

'Grace didn't like Andrew. There's a crack in the will about being satisfied that he can make whatever money he chooses; you could read it as a compliment, not, I assure you, meant that way. And Fiona's married to Gavin, who's rich as they come, you know. No need. She's got pin-money anyway. As for Annie, she's enough to see her out. That's just the outline, m'dear, we'll say no more today. Perhaps you'll be kind enough to come and see me in Edinburgh, we'll go over things in detail. Anything urgent, get in touch. Probate'll take ages of course, that needn't worry you.'

His voice took on a military, yet courtly, precision. She realized what it was. She was now the client, the genuinely esteemed one.

She said, 'I'm thinking of going abroad for a bit. Italy, but I'll come and see you before. Next week or the one after.'

'Perfect.'

He gives a nod and makes his way through the crowd towards Colin. She sees him take her brother by the elbow and they slip out of the side door into the little room which Grandpa Major called his library, though all he did there was smoke and snooze over the *Shooting Times*. She doesn't know quite how she feels. Rich—it's not a word she ever expected to apply to herself; it feels like a borrowed fur coat. Certainly something which will keep her warm, but . . . she supposes that when Alastair says rich, he means rich; it's not, she imagines, a word Edinburgh lawyers use loosely. How serpent-like of Grace, though she did hint in what was, stabbingly, almost the last thing she said. She had never acted rich. The rich are different from you and me, Ernest.

Not Grace. Yeah, Scott, they got more money—apparently that was just what Grace had had, and she, Belinda, now had also.

People were beginning to go away. It wasn't quite the sort of funeral that would turn into a wake, into a party. As the room cleared, Fiona's absence with Kevin would be noticed.

Upstairs, in a bed, in a darkened room that is not quite dark, Fiona mouth open, eyes staring, legs parted, calling hoarsely for the more Kevin is only too ready to give, Fiona redeeming years of aridity and self-denial, now saying a throaty 'yes' to her nature, what she has never admitted she wanted.

Belinda can see it so clearly, though she cannot see Kevin at all. He is, in her mind's eye and for Fiona, no more than an instrument. A force.

Diana is spoiling for a fight. She is like the old beat-up champ who won't admit he's through. I can still lick the world. But Diana is now a woman well on in life, whose mother is dead. She is nearer the grave than her last childbed, much much nearer. When you look close you can see that, in every way, the body is ready to give way. Two weeks ago, she could still pass for fifty, even on a good afternoon, less. Now she snaps at Belinda, snaps at Andrew, snubs Gavin, who is moonily eyeing the room as if Fiona was not doing what Belinda is sure she is doing. Diana snarls at Martin, who is white-faced and drinking whisky fast. When Colin comes in, she says, 'What the hell did you make us all go through that for?'

'Because it was the right shape,' says Colin.

Martin says to Belinda, 'Any chance of a word?'

'Let's go outside.'

The garden stretches before them tranquil and ordered, but there is a breath of autumn in the air and in the pale sky, now clear of clouds.

'Look,' Martin says, 'I'm sorry but I'm in a state. I must speak to someone and it's only you I can speak to. I'm sorry, Bel.'

She nods, nods and waits. They walk a bit, out of sight of the house, beyond the garden and into the trees.

'You'll have seen Jill wasn't there today.'

'Yes.'

'It's finished, bust-up.'

She doesn't know what to say, for he sounds distraught.

'You know there's been strain all summer.' He begins to laugh. He pulls out a gun-metal flask and takes a swig. 'Strain,' he says. 'I tried to stab her last night.'

'Oh God.' It is inadequate, what else could it be?

'She was going on and on and on and I picked up a knife.'

But if Martin wanted to stab Jill he would have no difficulty, so it didn't make sense.

'Anyway, I've got to get out. It can't go on.'

'But she's all right, I take it, you didn't actually do it, did you?'

'No. But next time, well, I might.'

They sit down on the wall, ignoring the damp. She wishes she had brought something warmer than the raincoat she picked up as they passed through the hall.

'I never really loved her, I suppose.'

'I used to think she loved you. She was . . . well more than that, I used to think.'

'Did you? She was jealous enough. I never really minded the jealousy, what I minded was the way she wanted to take me over. So, no . . . so when I said no to that we just, I suppose, drifted apart. It's all come to a head this summer, and now it's boiled over. I can't go back there tonight even.'

'Martin, she is all right, isn't she?'

She has this vision of Jill not being all right, and of Martin dressing in his morning-coat and black tie to come to Grace's funeral. It's absurd, there are, after all, the children too.

The silence lengthens. She looks away to her left, the light is failing and the pines are black against the pale sky. The faintest sliver of a moon can now be discerned against them.

She knows, with a finger-creeping knowledge, what Martin is asking for; and she can't give it.

'I've made all sorts of a fool of myself this summer—getting mixed up with the attempt to get rid of Mansie was one example.'

'I'd have thought that made sense. I can see a case for getting rid of Mansie.'

'Oh there's a case, but who the hell cares. And what is that political business anyway but an attempt to dodge things? Mansie's a clown, that's just what's needed.'

'So what are you going to do?'

Martin makes play with lighting a cigarette. He fingers the gun-metal flask he has laid on the dyke beside him. She catches from him a whiff she doesn't like; his jowls sag and his eyes are spaniel-moist in the half-light.

At last he says, in a half-voice, 'Thought I'd go away for a bit . . . I wondered if you'd made any plans yet.'

The temptation is there. Solutions always offer temptation. Only she knows what this solution would be worth. She daren't make another false start; is it naïve romanticism that says this would be one? She shakes her head. 'That's no use, Martin, for either of us.'

She won't take on a dependent; for a moment, she thinks of Kenneth, for a moment of shepherdesses and shepherd-lads in Arcady, resting against ruined Corinthian pillars, but no, that sort of dependency, that evasion, too, is out. And she won't put herself in a false position, as a position must be if it offers less than you are really prepared to settle for.

'I'm very fond of you, Martin, you know that. I'm going back to Italy, to Rome, I'm going to live there, I think. Come and see me there, stay for a bit if you like, but don't hope for anything more. I've nothing more to give you. Not now.'

His fingers tighten on the flask. The darkness deepens. The owl crosses the field. Back in the garden night-scented stock are fragrant. The river runs by Grace's grave, endless journeying to the sea.

V

With death and departures a chill crept over the house. There was a week of grey gusty mornings, the wind set in the east blowing up the valleys from the North Sea. Sky gave off a hard, grey, shadowless light; wind nipped leaves which were still green from the trees. Rain dashed against dirting window panes. The telephone was silent.

Colin, much in the kitchen, marked off departures in his mind. First, Belinda, the night sleeper to London, the 10.30 from Victoria to the Gare du Nord, taxi across Paris to the Gare de Lyon, and then the Palatino express to Rome; train which allowed her to waken to the benign folds and magic light of Umbria, landscape that is always, and yet never, for the first time.

Diana, back to London by aeroplane, alone. He couldn't remember seeing Diana alone; it was like a theatre set in the morning when the play is coming off. She wore a fur coat and there was no swagger, no allure in the wearing of it; Colin saw it worn as an animal wears it, for protection. He felt no pity. Kevin stayed a day or two after her departure. He hired a car and disappeared for hours. Belinda could have told Colin why; he didn't inquire. Then Kevin too turned his face to London and a new job, quickly arranged at Colin's expense over the telephone.

Annie with much flurry, ordering and cancelling of taxis, arranging this, rearranging that, went to stay at last with cousins in Carnoustie, pending the return of her house in Broughty Ferry. It might take time. She didn't speak to Colin after the funeral; that favouritism was at last burnt out, the death of seven or eight year old Colin finally admitted.

He saw nothing of Martin, nor of Patrick Craig. He assumed one farmed, the other doctored. Mansie Niven called in for a dram, announced he was off on an inter-Parliamentary visit to Guatemala.

A drenched September gave way to October. He went over to his sister's to shoot pheasants. Birds were few, rime glistened on the morning stubble and Gavin was distrait with drink. Only Fiona, with cool precision, brought off a left and right, accounting for half the day's bag. There was no talk of Morgan. Fiona had recovered from her misjudgement. It was rumoured he was in the South. Kwame on the other hand had found a job in a local grocer's and taken to drinking in the Graham Arms. Colin had bought him a few friendly beers and discussed racing form.

An election, much mooted, was postponed. Andrew would have to wait for his safe seat; Mansie had a few more months to make a fool of himself. It meant nothing to Colin.

He returned from Fiona's as the horizon shortened and cold mist rose heart-high in the haughland.

Away in London, in a cul-de-sac off the Earl's Court Road, Robin gave a Saturday night party. He sent an invitation to Colin who didn't of course reply, but Andrew came with a shy, correct boy from a Clearing Bank; Julie came with a young black dancer in a tangerine skirt; Sally came with three young men from Merchant Banks; Kenneth came alone in faded jeans, ragged sweater and an old army greatcoat.

'So you finally went to Cambridge, darling, did you?' said Andrew.

'Oh yes.'

'And how is it? Madly gay?'

'Up to a point. Actually it's a very light ale sort of place.'

'I did ask Colin and Belinda,' Robin assured everyone, 'but she's in Rome, and Colin didn't reply.'

'Oh Colin's hopeless,' Julie said, 'I didn't know you knew him. I didn't know anybody knew him.'

Belinda eats an avocado, spooning vinaigrette over the beach-sand flesh. Around her, even in October, tumble roses and profuse geraniums. Below and around, heat still comes

177

up from the terracotta roofs, infinitely varied in tone and shade, under the deep blue of the still unexpected sky. She stretches her legs, naked under the bathrobe, below the metal table so that toes catch the warming sun. She pushes the avocado aside and sips coffee, snake-eases herself from the table into the sunlight, and throws her head back, face and throat turned to the sun. She perches on the terrace wall, like one who cannot be there to stay, looking down and away over the roofs to the valley of the Tiber and the heights of the Janiculum beyond. If she turns her head to the right she can see the gleaming dome of St Peter's. She takes a flimsy letter from her bag which lies on the terrace wall beside her. The letter is from Kenneth and she collected it from Thomas Cook's yesterday afternoon.

'Have you heard from Belinda?' said Andrew. 'No, of course, you haven't. She's rich enough now to start living, not just in fantasy. You know that's just what you were to her, a fantasy, I won't say exactly of what kind, not in front of James here, he's ever so proper. Suburban-proper, you know, ducky.'

'No, I don't,' said Kenneth.

Belinda reads the little letter twice. Then her fingers close on it. It drops, crumpled, to the paving. She plucks a red rose from a strand that climbs over the terrace wall and hangs down. She presses the rose to her face, her fingers tightening on the petals. She lies on the mattress spread out on the terrace, letting her dressing-gown fall open. She draws up one knee and closes her eyes.

'Oh you needn't be concerned about me,' she had found herself saying to a friend the other day, 'I'm a rich woman now.'

'It's never been financial matters that's worried us about you, darling,' had been the reply.

She holds up her hand. The rose petals that are crushed

there flutter to the ground. There is no breeze and they fall straight, straight and singly.

Late at night there is dancing. Julie takes hold of Kenneth. She presses close against him.

'We've got something in common,' she says. 'You know what these Meldrums are, don't you? They're vampires, bloody vampires. They're short of their own blood. Do you understand what I'm saying? Colin's sucked me dry.'

'Oh yes, I suppose they're really just like the rest of us.'

'Oh God, you don't begin to understand.'

Kenneth smiles at this. 'Who wants to be understood?' he says. 'Which of us wouldn't cut his throat rather than be really understood?'

He smiles again; he is quoting what Colin once said to him.

'It's a hell of a bloody relationship,' says Julie.

'All relationships are that, there's always something killed. Colin once said to me all life was in *The Golden Bough*.'

'Very funny. He told me you could find it all in *Peter Rabbit*.'

'So you can,' says Kenneth, 'so in my experience you can.'

Belinda looks over the Lake at Nemi at the scene of dark violence where the macabre drama of *The Golden Bough* was enacted. She looks down steeply at the lake. The sun no longer strikes it and it lies pitch-black. Diana's temple has been replaced by greenhouses. She cannot form an image of the past. There are no priests, no broken columns, smell of blood or sacrifice. Merely the sun and the strawberries in a small Italian town. Even the museum is closed.

Yet, of course, it's all there. You are, she says to herself, what you are what you are, just like a rose.

She leaves the little square and begins to climb steep steps. Washing hangs across the narrows between the houses. Here too, roses and geraniums festoon the little terraces; other flowers hang from window-ledges. Old women in black dresses and head scarves sit, sit in the doorways, sometimes peeling vegetables into basins on the ground between their legs, sometimes knitting, but most often maybe, doing nothing but sit. Contentment comes up with heat from the stone. She emerges at a little white-washed church; whence comes thin sound of chanting. Perhaps it is a Saint's Day. Isn't it in fact always some saint's day? Children scurry about, barelegged, the odd dog mooches, cats snooze.

She sits on a broken wall and smokes a cigarette, the blue smoke quickly losing itself in the sky. The lake is out of sight here, all the classical associations dim. Only the hills to the left now catch the sun. A woman calls out to her children and three young girls come past, running. Belinda watches them out of sight behind the corner. Their voices come back at her for a bit till they lose themselves in the murmurs of the village. A cock crows, one of those Italian cocks that never know the time of day. It sets off another further down the hill.

She stubs out her cigarette with a little shiver. The sun hasn't yet disappeared, there is perhaps a half-hour of sunlight left, but she is for the first time that afternoon reminded that it is October.

She picks up the bag she has laid on the wall beside her and walks down the hill, out of sun into shadow. The lake is no longer visible from the terrace, a mist is rising from the water.

Colin opened the car's boot and took out the glass case which contained the peacock. He was glad he had at last remembered it was ready. He carried it into the house, into the old morning-room that he now called the study, not that there was anyone else to use the name or that he studied there. Still it was the room with leather arm-chairs and a log fire where, having abandoned the kitchen, he spent most of his waking time. In fact, it wasn't unusual for him to sleep there too, and wake grey, shivering and dirty-mouthed, in the deep leather arm-chair that had been his grandfather's.

He cleared a space on the table and set the case down. The job had been well done. The bird retained its panoply of finery, yet didn't at all suggest it was anything more, in any way, than a stuffed peacock in a case. He admired it from all angles.

'Let observation with extensive view
Survey mankind from China to Peru,' he said.

He poured himself a half-tumbler of whisky from the tantalus. You were all right, axiomatically all right, as long as you continued to decant your whisky. It was when you got to drinking straight from the bottle's neck that it was time to worry. He carried the glass to the window and looked out on the withered garden. In November all gardens were ghosts.

Rain coursed down the window, mist hung heavy on trees and bushes, damp seeped into the stones and woodwork, stained the fabric of the house, turned the lawn sour sedge-yellow. Colin turned away with a sigh, glanced at the silent television set (no racing today), passed under the engraving of the 'Charge of the Scots Greys at Waterloo' and settled himself in the arm-chair. He began to read an account of the second Afghan War, selected from a pile of books on the side-table. A good many dealt with Imperial India, and there were volumes of Surtees and Ouida and Evelyn Waugh, and the official history of his old school. After a bit he pushed aside the Afghan War—it looked as if the limits of Empire had been reached, at least in that direction—and picked up the school history. *Pietas et gravitas; vero Romano.* There were choice letters in which one of the Victorian headmasters rebuked a parent (holding the sad rank of major) for failing to return his son in time for evening chapel. The chapel, said the worthy doctor, is at the heart of school life; without attendance at chapel, boys cannot be expected to develop the proper frame of dutiful mind. Doubtless it was true. This is the chapel; here, my son, your father thought the thoughts of youth, and heard the words, ti-tum, ti-tum, the touch of life has turned to truth. The touch of life; quite a phrase. The merest touch of life. How did it end? . . .

'Qui procul hinc', the legend's writ,—
The frontier-grave is far away—
'Qui ante diem periit:
Sed miles, sed pro patria.'

Unfashionable, of course, but fine enough, if . . . if you could only believe. Rank unbelief is sure to err . . . what had the touch of life to say to that? But . . . but there was also Arnold, the school inspector himself, we others pine and wish the long unhappy dream would end. The long unhappy . . .

There was a knocking at the door.

'Who's there?'

It opened to admit Martin.

'Would you say that was true?' Colin said.

'What was true?'

'Do you wish the long unhappy dream would end? True for you?'

'I'm lost. What are you talking about?'

'Matthew Arnold.'

'Oh.'

Martin was looking better. He had a new rhythm in his step.

'I'm not with you,' he said.

'Aren't you? I was talking about this strange disease of modern life, but let it pass, let it pass, like the hounds of spring. Would you, instead, care for a drink?'

'Why not?'

'You're looking bobbish.'

'I've been making some arrangements, got Jill out.'

'You have, good.'

Colin had levered himself from his chair and was pouring Martin a strongish drink. He limped back with it.

'Cost you a bit, I expect,' he said.

'I'll be up shit creek for life, but it's worth it.'

They settled themselves in chairs, opposite each other, cousins, in a sense brothers.

'She's actually going to move?' said Colin.

'She's actually going to move, yes.'

'So your famous question, how does a farmer leave his wife, resolves itself. He pays.'

'He pays.'

'Money, as the great lady said, is how it is done. Money is just how things are done.'

'That's the way it is. And you? How goes the struggle?'

'*Ça va.* I've been doing a bit of thinking, always tough going. About the death of Empire, and, rather oddly, Suez.'

'Oh Empire, Suez, that's all past politics.'

'Absolutely, but also present . . . present discontents.'

'I'm not with you. You've lost me again.'

'The death of will . . . the ideal of service . . . all gone.'

'Exaggeration, surely.'

'Well I won't argue with you, but without it, what are we thrown back on? Private selfishness, money-making . . .'

'Nothing wrong with making money. In my opinion. What though's the point of that?' He indicated the peacock.

'Oh symbolism, nothing but symbolism.'

'I see. Morbid, a bit morbid.'

There was a long silence, perhaps brooding on morbidity or evanescence of all things, the urn burial view of life; perhaps empty.

'Heard from Bel?' said Martin at last.

'A couple of letters. She says she's writing something, maybe even a book.'

'Writing a book . . . do you know, it'll probably be good.'

'Perhaps—no reason why not. Not, I imagine, so terribly difficult. Think after all of the shits who bring it off, but still . . . Christ.'

'Anything else? Any word of coming home?'

'No, no, nothing at all really.'

'Mansie went to see her, you know. He was in Rome on some European nonsense. He told me she was making a mistake, probably told her too. Mansie could hardly resist. But I expect that means he proposed to her. Mansie's always had a thing about Bel. I suppose that may have been one reason why I couldn't stand him.'

'You've made it up then?' said Colin.

'Yes, I suppose so, in the end, no reason why not.'

'Want the fire on? It's getting chilly.'

'No, don't feel it. Must be off anyway, just looked in to see how you were. Got a phone number for Bel, by any chance?'

'No.'

'I suppose International Enquiries'll be able to trace it. Care of who?'

'Steinbeck. You've got the address?'

'Via Gregoriana 47, yes? I think this time we'll fix it. Time we did.'

'Well, you might. I wouldn't know.'

'Might is right. I don't mean that, I mean I wouldn't put it higher than might.'

Martin stood up, kicking his legs from the knees.

'We've all had a terrible summer,' he said. 'Traumatic, not that that's a word I care to use. Trendy nonsense. But still, Grace's death, marriage bust-ups and so on. Time for re-orientation now. I know Bel had a sort of thing for young Kenneth in the summer, it was obvious, wasn't it, but that sort of thing doesn't really count. That sort of affair's just evasion. So . . . we'll see. I'll get in touch anyway. We belong together. I've always known it. Trouble was, originally, at the time it might all have worked out easily, I got it all wrong. Put her on a pedestal, that sort of thing. No good. Still, you live and learn.'

Colin gave a little shrug. 'I wouldn't know,' he said.

Martin gathered himself. 'I've talked to Patrick Craig about it. He understands Bel pretty well, in fact I thought for a bit he was after her, but no. Patrick's not going to commit himself again. What he said was, she's a girl who really needs children. And it's true, without children, what have you in life? No real decency, nothing to hold on to. I know that with mine, even if they are also Jill's. So. Patrick also said her feeling for Kenneth was quasi-maternal.'

'I wouldn't know,' Colin said again. He lit a cigarette. 'I just wouldn't know.'

'I was nearly off my rocker,' said Martin. 'I know that now. Thing to remember is you can always come back. It's not like boxing.'

'Oh yes,' said Colin.

He watched Martin drive away and stood on the gravel listening till the sound of the car's engine died in the distance. Then he followed him down the back drive. He swung the heavy gate round into position and bolted it and fastened and locked the padlock. For a moment he rested his arms on the top bar, looking across the road to fields of stubble that ran uphill to meet the lowering laden sky. Two or three crows picked their delicate way among the stubble. There was no wind at all. Rainwater from the bare branches dripped straight to the roadway.

Colin turned to see that Peter Begg had come out of the cottar house to the left of the gates and was standing in his garden, among the wet stalks of kail. With his pipe still in his mouth, he said, 'Aye, it's a soft day, Colin.'

'Soft enough.'

'But we'll have an early winter, I saw the geese flying this morn.'

'It wouldn't surprise me.'

He raised a hand, rejecting all possibility of surprise, and turned in a moment off the drive, into the bushes that fringed it, following a path that led, a short-cut, through a rough wood. But the years had encroached on the path. The way, well-known in childhood, was lost. He had to push branches of rhododendron aside, and dying bracken twisted round his feet. Under the branches it was very dark, and when he emerged, he saw that day was departing from the heavy sky.